Mahasweta Devi (1926–2016) was one of our foremost literary personalities, a prolific and bestselling author in Bengali of short fiction and novels; a deeply political social activist who worked with and for tribal people and marginalized communities like the landless labourers of eastern India for years; the editor of a quarterly, *Bortika*, in which the tribal people and marginalized peoples themselves documented grassroots-level issues and trends; and a socio-political commentator whose articles appeared regularly in the *Economic and Political Weekly*, *Frontier* and other journals.

Mahasweta Devi made important contributions to literary and cultural studies in this country. Her empirical research into oral history as it lives in the cultures and memories of tribal communities was a first of its kind. Her powerful, haunting tales of exploitation and struggle have been seen as rich sites of feminist discourse by leading scholars. Her innovative use of language has expanded the conventional borders of Bengali literary expression. Standing as she does at the intersection of vital contemporary questions of politics, gender and class, she is a significant figure in the field of socially committed literature.

Recognizing this, we have conceived a publishing programme which encompasses a representational look at the complete Mahasweta: her novels, her short fiction, her children's stories, her plays, her activist prose writings. The series is an attempt to introduce her impressive body of work to a readership beyond Bengal; it is also an overdue recognition of the importance of her contribution to the literary and cultural history of our country.

SEAGULL BOOKS
•
CELEBRATING
40 YEARS

THE INDIA LIST

MAHASWETA DEVI

TRUTH/UNTRUTH

Translated by Anjum Katyal

LONDON CALCUTTA NEW YORK

Seagull Books, 2023

Originally published in Bengali as *Satya-Asatya* in 1986

Currently available in *Mahasweta Devi Rachanasamagra*, VOL. 13

[Collected works of Mahasweta Devi] (2004)

© Tathagata Bhattacharya

First published in English translation by Seagull Books, 2023

English translation © Anjum Katyal, 2023

ISBN 978 1 80309 077 1

British Library Cataloguing-in-Publication Data

A catalogue record for this book is available from the British Library

Typeset by Seagull Books, Calcutta, India

Printed and bound by WordsWorth India, New Delhi, India

CONTENTS

ONE

For those who gasp at the mere mention of Khidirpur, it is to make them gasp in yet another way that high-rise building after building keeps shooting up. 'These concrete jungles of today / Where humans like mere insects stay / No chance for love, no chance to play' definitely no longer applies to these homes.

Many-storeyed buildings, many inhabitants, many loves, all kinds of games, they have it all.

One such building is Barnamala.

Multi-storeyed. Divided into six blocks. When you come in, it's as if you've entered a small city.

A large park in front, with three blocks on three sides. A similar park at the back, with three identical blocks. Promoters are environment polluters. Greenery is a must: they know, they understand. So all along Barnamala Apartments' very high boundary walls you'll see eucalyptus and debdaru trees. Ivy creepers climb the walls. In the parks, too, a wonderful profusion of trees.

And to keep the children happy, all kinds of animal shapes made of twisted wire frames and greenery, elephants and horses and what not. Plus special areas for them in both parks.

The name 'Barnamala' is not really appropriate. But even promoters are susceptible to the magic of the Arabian Nights with their mysterious boxes that open to reveal another box. And another inside that.

The promoters too are quite an Arabian mystery. The one they call 'boss' is not really the boss. The real boss is in the background, silent.

But he is not a man lacking in refinement. He wants a name, a new kind of name, and is driving the others crazy about it. Finally, his secretary says: Why are you so worried?

–What do you mean, why am I worried? Is naming a building such an easy matter? Doesn't one have to give it some thought?

–Boudi says she will consult Guruji, he will suggest a name.

–Yes, I know. The name must begin with B.

Actually, his own home is called Baisakhi, his garden house Bichitra, his Park Street office Baruna. Guruji's name is Barabhoyananda Swami, He-Who-Gifts-One-Freedom-from-Fear. So without B there can be no salvation.

Reaching Barabhoyananda is very difficult. If he's here today, he's in Italy tomorrow. In summer he's in France, in winter in Greece. If you go to his Kolkata office, he communicates via telex message, his devotees' only recourse. His 'office' is a huge, glass-walled flat on the eleventh floor of one of his disciples' buildings. Every floor has six flats. The eleventh has just one. And a garden. A small swimming pool, a swing, everything. It is with Barabhoyananda's help and some string pulling in Delhi that this almost-sunk-by-a-chit-fund disciple has managed to establish an import–export business and somehow build this house on Circular Road. A house in Delhi. A hotel in Darjeeling. Thus he ekes out a humble living.

Hence, the eleventh floor was given to Gurudeb. And it is to that eleventh floor that the telex message came: 'Barnamala'.

And that is how Barnamala—'Alphabet'—got its name. Actually, the real boss was hoping that the people who lived there would have names from A to Z, but that didn't happen. It would have been so poetic. But those who can part with four to seven lakh rupees for a flat there had not been named with poetics in mind. Can one have it all? One makes do with whatever one gets.

The real promoter also wanted that just as A-babu had named his flat Avantika, the others too would name their flats accordingly.

Not everyone did. Still, Harnam Malhotra named his flat Halanga, after his native village. And Mr U called his flat Barisal Glory.

Not one of them had a poetic sensibility. Just the thought of it fills the real promoter with sorrow. He has reserved three flats on the topmost floor of Block One. He spends a night there every now and then, counts the stars and ponders the future of the nation.

This is the kind of building in which everyone is supposed to be happy.

Yet something went terribly wrong.

TWO

And of all places, in Avantika.

Avantika was A-babu's flat. A-babu's wife was Kumkum. In this building, it wasn't the practice to be really friendly with one another. A-babu and Kumkum even less so. Kumkum did not feel that any of her neighbours was sufficiently cultured. An MA in philosophy. She could spend hour after hour lecturing on the true meaning of culture.

Forget other people, she'd tell even her own husband: You have no culture.

What can A-babu say? It is true, he does not understand the virtuosity of sitar maestro Ravi Shankar in quite the same way as does Kumkum's sister-in-law Bhaswati's brother. He can't appreciate Ramkinkar's sculpture like Kumkum's maternal cousin Ruma, nor Jamini Roy's paintings. And because he can't understand Picasso's art even today, his brother-in-law's wife Bhaswati never fails to humiliate him.

A-babu sits silently when they talk of all this. Of course, with a slight smile pinned to his lips. Culture-vulture!

Bhaswati's brother, their Barnamala neighbour's son Joyraj, Ruma, they're all culture vultures. From the Kolkata Book Fair to photography shows, from dhokra exhibitions to contemporary Hindi plays, from flower shows to Nandan film festivals, how feverishly they rush to and fro.

The women all look alike, dress alike, and so do the men.

A-babu laughs to himself.

You're watching so much, listening to so much, but are you understanding any of it? To think, to understand—where is the time for that?

Nowadays, nobody had the time, no time, no time to spare. After giving it much thought, A-babu had decided that even if he paid them no attention, he was and would be just fine.

A-babu knows only too well that any brain power expended on trying to figure out Third Theatre was a waste of time. He may not know about Third Theatre, yet he was still an intelligent man.

After all, had he been poor at studies? No, he'd been quite good. Not that he dwelt any more on his student days. Those who are so busy with the present, how will they think of the past? Where is the time?

Kumkum had never wanted to know either.

She has married a successful and wealthy contractor. She has no interest in his life before they wed. A-babu sometimes thinks, Such is the rule of Time. Who wants to return to the past, to clear the fallen leaves off the dew-drenched moonlit forest floor and uncover traces of a path? *Oh flower-filled forest path . . .* that song comes back to him now and then.

These days, every time you meet someone new, it's as if everything begins from that very moment. It's a sign of the times. A-babu understands this and has adapted to the need of the hour.

He'd been good at his studies. Had an analytical mind.

His teachers would say: Get into research. You'll go to the top.

–No sir, I won't be able to.

–You will.

–There's no money in it.

That was the one mistake he'd made in his calculations. Researchers today, even research students, have it really good. After your studies, you can go abroad. Get a job in an Indian university or research institute. Hold seminar after seminar.

Even though A-babu's friend Subhendu had written, I'll come one day, we'll eat muri-beguni together, raw-mango chutney, he still hasn't had the time to visit. Flying from Melbourne to Paris, Minnesota to Geneva, poor fellow barely has time to land.

A-babu did not go into research, he joined a contractor's office and learnt the trade.

A seeking mind, a researcher's mind. That such a mind, even when applied to a contractor's job, can yield gold: A-babu is proof of this.

Different projects are acquired under different names. A-babu stays in the background. Such handling of tenders and bill collection needs real talent.

His teachers said, Become a teacher. It's because he hadn't that today, in his office-with-no-name, he employs at least ten people, each of whom is paid double the salary of a college lecturer.

Calcutta currently is an ocean of money. From constructing the Metro rail to levelling the Dhapa wastelands, from building bridges to building hospitals, whatever you got into, there was money to be made.

A-babu's name is Arjun Chakravarty. Wicked people said that his real name was Sanatan Pushilal. But because that name was not sufficiently attractive, he had changed it to a nicer one. He had named himself.

*

Today, something went terribly wrong at home.

Ten years have passed since he got married. In all that time, Kumkum has not had a child. It's not as if she and A-babu had been unwilling. Yet she had not conceived. Did thatmake her unhappy?

It was hard to tell.

Yet, every so often she would say, What's the use of all this money? Who will we leave it to, what will we do with it? Who are we collecting all this for?

Arjun would say, Be patient. Keshtokali has said you are sure to bear a child.

Keshtokali is a kabiraj, a renowned Ayurvedic practitioner. With a very successful practice. No one other than the two of them knows the history of his friendship with Arjun-babu. Once upon a time, Arjun-babu's uncle used to supply leaves and roots to Keshtokali Kabiraj's father.

That poor and timid man one day begged Shastri-moshai: Babu, so many have food to eat because of you. Can you give some shelter to my nephew? He's very good at his studies. But no mother or father. How much more can I do for him?

7

The elderly kabiraj was an old-fashioned man. The ground floor of his home already housed a few such needy young men who were pursuing their studies.

–All right, bring him along.

That is how Sanatan came into his home. How Sanatan became Arjun. And how, erasing the past, Arjun slowly rode the lift of high aspirations all the way up to the twelfth floor of society . . . all that is but ancient history now.

The old kabiraj did not live to see Arjun's success. Keshtokali is the sole surviving link to his past.

Kumkum, though, doesn't have much faith in Ayurveda. She has never been able to truly accept it.

Yet, that incredible incident did take place. And today Kumkum is eight months pregnant. Currently staying at her father's. She needs plenty of looking after at a time like this. And Arjun is hardly ever at home.

Kumkum will be safe in her mother's care. Arjun-babu is not worried, not worried at all.

Nor is he worried about whether it'll be a boy or a girl. If it's a boy, nothing like it. The empire he's built up brick by brick—he'll leave it all to him.

And if it's a girl?

She'll get it all too. And because she'll get it all, she won't die a mysterious death at her in-laws'. He'll prepare her well.

This is what he thinks about these days. What he was thinking about today as well. Who could have thought that the maid Jamuna would come in just then, give him such terrible news?

Jamuna lived in a slum in this controversial neighbourhood. There are many reasons why this area bordering the docks is so controversial. Rumour has it that here, even the common man is involved in some form of anti-social activity. But can the residents of multi-storey apartment blocks like Barnamala afford to worry about such things? They need servants, after all.

Shiny modern flats filled with the latest gadgets and appliances. The pictures one sees of high-society homes on television, in advertisements, in the movies, are just like the kitchens, living rooms, bedrooms in these flats.

The mistresses of such homes don't do any household chores. This society, in its attempt to be like the West, has aped its outward appearance to perfection.

But not its inner attitudes.

In the West, most people don't have domestic help. Husbands and wives share the chores—but the upper echelons of this country don't accept this.

In their hearts, each one is landed gentry.

They want a maid, they want a houseboy, they want a cook, they want it a–l–l. Not a single one wants to help with the housework.

Hence, the nearby slums to the rescue.

What are the residents of all these multi-storeys to do, after all? They know these people are suspect, yet they employ them.

But they're nervous. So they need a security service. Twenty-four-hour guards.

Barnamala too has such an arrangement.

Which is why Arjun-babu is not worried, not worried at all. His house is filled with locker after locker. Expensive brands of lockers. Before the cash is deposited into anonymous accounts, it is stored at home. Nothing to worry about.

There is a security service, after all.

But what is all this that Jamuna is saying?

–Babu!

–What is it, Jamuna?

–Have to talk.

–To me?

In her nylon sari and backless blouse (given by Kumkum), a furious Jamuna glares at him with furious eyes.

–If not you, then who?

–You're talking to me like this?!

–I'll talk to you as I like, what can you do about it? You bastard, you damn devil!

–Chhi chhi! Shame on you, Jamuna!

–Boudi goes away and you start fooling around with me! Didn't think about all this, then?

–Hush, Jamuna, not so loud!

–You know what's happened to me?

–What's happened?

Jamuna places her hands on her belly in a telling gesture and looks at him.

–You're . . . you're . . .

–Yes, yours.

–How long?

–Since Boudi left. Barely seven months when you got rid of her. Now you sit and count.

Arjun-babu feels faint.

–Jamuna! What are you saying?!

–Don't you know what I'm saying? My husband hasn't come to me for so long. You forced yourself on me . . . no one else has the guts to lay a finger on me. Now you better sort it out.

–Me? I have to . . .

–Then who?

–Why should I?

–Think you'll get out of it? You don't know Jamuna. Where I live, there're plenty of gangs. If I spill the beans—do you know what'll happen to you? When an old cock sprouts new feathers, this is his fate. Got your wife with child in your ripe old age, but you can't rest till you've spoilt the maids!

Arjun was astonished by her reference to the 'old cock'. Had Jamuna read the Michael Madhusudhan play?

–So what you thinking, babu?

–Look Jamuna, what's done is done . . .

–You have to pay me.

–Jamuna, have you read Michael?

–You making fun of me?

–Pay you? Why? I'll take you, I mean, you'll go, I'll arrange everything.

–No, babu. Jamuna's not such a fool.

–What do you mean?

–You'll say hospital but you'll take me somewhere else, kill me, I know everything. I know you babus very well.

–Chhi, chhi! Shame, shame, Jamuna. You think I—

Arjun-babu is deeply wounded. It's all Kumkum's fault. Watching Jamuna do the housework, her lush body clad in the pretty saris and blouses that Kumkum had given her, that's what's led to . . .

–I know you only too well!

–Listen, I'll get you some medicine.

–Medicine will do the trick?

–Definitely.

–All right, bring it. Now hand over the money.

–What do you need the money for?

–If the medicine fails, I'll go to nurse-didi. Won't she take money?

–How much?

–For now, one thousand rupees.

–Do I have that kind of cash on me?

–Eh, you corpse-chewing maggot! Who're you trying to fool? What about that loft in the bathroom, with the safe in the wall? And those big sacks of cash that lie around for days? Don't even bother to put them in the locker?

–You've . . . you've seen them?

–Many times.

–Wait.

Jamuna counts out the cash. Then says, If you think you'll accuse me of being a thief, just know that your wife'll be made a widow. You don't know my brothers. Two brothers, two goons. They'll finish you for sure, for sure.

–No, no, I won't accuse you.

–When it's finished, I'll rest here a few days, eat well. Boudi isn't coming back in a hurry, I know.

Leaving behind a stunned Arjun-babu, Jamuna languidly makes her way out.

Arjun-babu sits with his head in his hands. Disaster! Disaster! Calamity in Barnamala. This is meant to be an auspicious time for him, the next eight years are supposed to go well, then what's this Jamuna's just told him?

He tries to think. While Jamuna's raw physicality and turbulent youth are true, it is also true that Kumkum had been unable to conceive all these years. Was it the kabiraj's medicine that had enhanced his virility? Is that why all this has happened?

He debates silently with himself. He is scared. Very scared.

–What are you scared of, Arjun?

–What if Jamuna tells everyone?

–So what if she does?

–Don't I have an image in society?

–Forget it. In your society, if a maid is ruined or killed, your image isn't affected in the least. Your social standing remains unchanged.

–What if Kumkum finds out?

13

–Nothing will happen. Many Kumkums have found out, yet they continue to keep house for their Arjuns. Money rules women, don't you know?

–Jamuna knows about the cash.

–So what. You also pay for the security service.

–She mentioned her brothers . . .

–Pay off the police, the police will fix them.

–I'm scared.

–Don't be scared.

Arjun shouts 'Don't be scared!' Then he remembers Keshtokali.

One thousand rupees is nothing. Arjun-babu pays many more thousands in bribes to secure his projects. But that a maid should make off with a thousand rupees, this he simply cannot tolerate.

Was Jamuna telling the truth or lying? What if she didn't fix it? What if she got him into trouble? No, he must go to Keshtokali. Tell him everything.

THREE

There's no end to Jamuna's worries either. It may appear incredible to everyone, but she still feels a deep love for her absent husband Moloy. All the time she thinks, Moloy will come back. What if he comes back now? How will she explain that she went astray just this one time? Lost in thoughts of you, I forgot everything else, then when babu . . . the body has its own needs, after all . . . can't one's foot slip just the once?

Given that she belongs to the slum, this love of Jamuna's seems slightly unreal.

Because Johnny and Tala aren't really her brothers. Nobody is anybody's brother here. Nobody is anybody's sister. Yet they share an incredible bond.

Johnny and Tala are complete anti-socials. They spend their days in theft and petty crime.

Jamuna too had been one of them. After she started working at Barnamala, they had burgled three homes. Since Jamuna had given them the leads, they'd given her a share of the loot.

That's why Moloy used to say, Leave this life. Come away, we'll work hard, earn an honest living. He was a good man. Yes, a very good man, Moloy. But you were the factory's blow man. When the factory shut down, what new job did you get?

You got nothing. You went away saying you'd find a job, then you'd come and fetch me.

Johnny and Tala are doing just fine.

They're looking for more money. As capital. As soon as they get it, they'll leave, go somewhere else, to some other city. Both have another, more socially acceptable identity: one is a plumber, the other an electrician. They know everyone quite well at the Barnamala office, that is, at the caretaker's office.

Which is why they do occasional odd jobs in these flats too.

Jamuna thinks of them as she makes her way home.

They've been telling her for a while now: Just let us know where babu keeps what. Tell us. We do the job. Split the cash. Then who cares if you and Moloy live like king and queen? You have a dream, want to open a hotel. We also want to go somewhere else, find work. Just tell us.

–Big plans. But if you get caught?

–Hah, who knows where we're going with the money? The office-babu, durwan, liftman, we know them all, they'll all get a share. Who'll catch us?

Arjun and his kind, they're helpless, helpless, yet they don't know it. The very caretaker's office they trust is full of thieves. They don't know, so they think all is well.

Jamuna frets and fidgets. I can get into trouble too, can't I?

–With us around, can trouble touch you?

–No trouble, you're sure?

–Arrey, don't we know people in that office? If they catch you, just see what we do. And who'll catch you? That babu? Arjun-babu? Oh, what an Arjun he is. That fat slob, one nudge and he'll fall over. One thing, though, does babu keep a dog?

–No. Boudi can't stand dogs.

*

Once she got back home, Jamuna first made sure she stashed the cash safely, then sent for Johnny and Tala.

–Listen, I have something to tell you.

Eyes downcast, Jamuna speaks slowly and softly. Tears flow down her cheeks.

Johnny and Tala are astounded.

Johnny says, But why're you crying? You ran away from the orphanage, then bit the tout's hand and ran away from him. Never seen you cry. If you're crying now, it must be because of Moloy.

–If he finds out . . .

Tala growls, What'll he do? Cut off your head? If you leave behind your married wife and roam about all the time . . .

Johnny says, Who'll offer your wife potecshun, huh? He ever think about that?

Jamuna laughs. Why, didn't he give that job to you? Tell you to watch out for me?

–He did, and we did too. But really, Jamuna, you've gone too far. These saris, these blouses!

17

–The babus are insulted if we wear cotton saris to work.

–Now what's to be done?

–As long as we have Lame Doctor, what's the worry?

Like neighbourhood, like doctor. Whether Lame Doctor even has a medical degree, what his qualifications are, no one worries about all that. One day Peter Sadhu brought him here and set him up.

Peter was not his first name, nor was Sadhu his surname. He wore saffron clothes, had taken control of the neighbourhood. That was the time of Joy Bangla. Peter was a mastaan from that time.

Improvement of slums and roads, of water and electric supply—the vote-seeking babus used to come and make all these promises. Peter would sit at home and laugh at them. Won't happen, nothing will happen. You want this area to stay steeped in crime. You want the slum dwellers to rot and die in their slums. Why else will you follow the 'do whatever anyone says' policy?

You won't improve the roads. Police vans swooping in, picking up thecriminals—you certainly don't want that to happen. You lot are also the ones behind Peter Sadhu.

Water? Electricity? Are there any funnier words than these? In the poor neighbourhoods, you've never set up water taps or electric poles and connections, and you never will. They'll run on stolen electricity, everyone knows that.

Though, yes, a doctor is necessary. But a smart, clever, freshly qualified doctor, who wants one of those? What's needed is a doctor who can get the job done.

Like neighbourhood, like job.

He was the one who brought in and set up Lame Doctor. The neighbourhood needed just such a doctor. To dig out bullets, stitch up knife wounds, prescribe contraceptives, abortion medicines, and so on. The fevers, infections, injuries, children's stomach upsets, all of that too, of course.

Certain powerful medicines had to be kept in stock as well. That which mixed with alcohol can put one to sleep forever.

Paid off by Raja, Lame Doctor himself gave precisely such a medicine to Peter Sadhu one day.

No, as long as Lame Doctor was there, Jamuna didn't have to worry.

–But the medicine that babu wants to give me?

–Arrey, silly! Lame Doctor's medicine will do the trick. Didn't you take it once before?

–That was my one big sin, my dear! How Moloy tried to stop me. Said, We're married, why do you want to do this? But I didn't listen, did I?

–But he'd just lost his job!

–That was why. We know.

–How did it help? He got so upset, left home in a rage. If only I had listened to him.

–Forget it. It's over and done with.

–Listen, after taking the medicine, I'll go back there. Enter through the bathroom. I have a key. It's attached to a bedroom. Babu's not there most of the time, the house is empty.

–What if he kills you?

–Then you'll go and catch him!

–Where does he keep the cash?

–In the bathroom lopt.

–For how long?

–Two–four days, then he moves it. There's also a locker in the lopt. There too . . .

–How will we know?

–I'll tell you for sure.

–Sure?

–Sure. And if you see that I haven't come back home, you'll know that babu has caught me. Then you go and do whatever you can.

–Does he know about us?

–I said you were my brothers.

–You know what's best? You take Lame Doctor's medicine, then go there and rest. We'll go and threaten babu, take the cash and then bring you back home. And that's it. Done.

–All right.

–Babu doesn't have a chamber, does he?

–No, no, he's scared of guns.

–But he stores so much cash at home?

–Who doesn't, in that place?

–Isn't there a security service?

–Yes, there is.

–Then?

–Don't irritate me, Johnny. The guards are at the front. They patrol the entrances. You'll enter from the back, use the sweeper's stairs. I'll keep that entrance unlocked.

–We'll do the job and clear out.

–I'll go off to Puri. Open a small hotel there. Enough for the two of us to live on.

–Moloy and you.

–You two guys will be fine.

–And why not! We're the temporary ones. The temporaries of this life. Marriage, etc., is only for the permanents. Who wants to be a permanent? Is there any lack of women in this world?

–That's true.

–When is Moloy back?

–Only he knows.

–Jamuna! You work in other flats too. Isn't it possible there . . . ?

–Don't be greedy, Tala. I work in four homes, true, but burglary in those four will mean my arrest for sure. And if the police get me, they'll get you too.

–That's true.

–This house is the most convenient. Everyone does part-time work and leaves. The other flats have staff that stays day and night. This is the best, even the wife's not there.

–OK. As you say, so it shall be. But what about money for you too, from your babu . . .

–Get it out of him if you can.

–Listen, Jamuna. Your . . . condition . . . it isn't too advanced, is it? If so, tell us, we'll take you to a hospital . . .

–No, no, just about—

–They've named the building Bannamala!

–Not Bannamala—Barnamala! A for apple, B for ball . . . It's not a building, it's Indrapuri. Every bathroom has hot water, cold water, seventeen kinds of soap, shampoo, hair dye, stacks of towels!

–Many others work there too—

Jamuna falls about laughing. She can really laugh; there's something childlike about her when she does. Chortling, she says, They give falso names and work there. Nepal, Mohsin, Abed, Sabita, all of them!

–If you make such buildings in a place like Khidirpur, who else will work for you? Saints and sages?!

–Exactly!

–The police turn a blind eye.

–Everything's running on deals and money.

Jamuna sighs. Even if you loot all the flats, the sin is the same. At No. 7, the driver ran off with a lakh of rupees. The office called the police. I was mopping the floors, I heard the babu telling the police, Let it go, let it go. The police let it go, but they jerked him around first. Do you think it's only money? So much more goes on there!

–For them, all sins are forgiven.

–Anyway, I've told you all I know. Whatever you do, don't go shedding any blood now.

–Do we ever?

–One chop from Johnny and that's the end of babu.

–No, no, I don't do karate.

–I'm very scared of blood.

–Really! You're changing, Jamuna. Like that movie, you're becoming domesticated. Haven't you seen plenty of blood these ten years?

–Yes, I have but it still scares me.

–No, no, we'll do a clean job, just take the money, leave. Go somewhere far away and set up shop.

–I'll also go away.

–If you leave Moloy, you can come with us.

–I can never leave him. That's why he keeps saying, Let's work hard, earn an honest living.

–When Moloy comes, we'll make sure he leaves with you.

–Look. He lost his factory job, and I did him wrong. He left. Still, he keeps coming back. How many times he told me, Leave this bad lot, Jamuna. Leave your get-rich-quick dreams. I would say, By bad lot do you mean Johnny and Tala? They've watched over me for years, saved me from so many others. I've made them my brothers. They got me married.

–You have no one, it was our duty to get you married. You're the one who fell madly in love!

–He doesn't understand all that.

–He's different. How he got involved with you . . . I've taken a sniff of him, he smells like a decent man. And now you're becoming a good housewife too.

–What rubbish you talk.

23

–It won't work, Jamuna. We can never be decent. Whenever we try, it ends in disaster.

–Let it be. I'll go to Lame Doctor, but I hope that having smoked his daily pot or taken his tablets he won't give me the wrong thing? He's started making mistakes these days.

–Why should he make a mistake? Just that day Moyna . . .

–No, no, it will be fine. I saw a beautiful bird this morning! My heart tells me he's bound to come, if not today then tomorrow. Let him come. Then I'll tell him, Let's go away. Go to Puri and open a small hotel. That's also an honest path, an honest living.

–What will you do in the hotel?

–Wear a maxi and sit at the counter and total the bills? Do I know reading and writing enough for that? A hotel needs so many other kinds of work to be done. I was at one for some time.

–Yes, I remember.

–OK, we've talked a lot. Now I need to go out, get the medicine.

Johnny and Tala leave. Jamuna retrieves the cash carefully. Brothers or not, they would surely have wanted a share.

*

Lame Doctor's medicine makes you uneasy. Fills the body with pain. That's why Jamuna will go back to Arjun-babu's flat. The bathroom she enters from is attached to the guest bedroom. That's where she'll lie down and rest.

The part-timers in that house are Mohini and Bahadur. Jamuna knows them both well. Once babu leaves, they all eat the fish, meat, butter, bread. Mohini takes away oil, ghee, rice, dal, sugar.

Bahadur takes away bottles of liquor and sells them.

Jamuna does none of that. She goes into the bathroom, uses the soaps and shampoos her hair to her heart's content. Puts on perfume.

If she led as pampered a life as Boudi, what a beauty Jamuna would have been!

Anyway, no point thinking about Barnamala. Let Moloy come, Jamuna will go off somewhere or other. Just look at Jamuna's luck! All her life she spent one way. And then she met Moloy, and then see what happened!

Her heart tells her that all will be well.

FOUR

Arjun-babu has, of course, left already, to go and meet Keshtokali Kabiraj. An old habit. To rush to him in times of trouble. A very old habit.

From when they both sat side by side every morning for breakfast before going to school, from when they both joined college, Keshtokali knew that one day he would have to take over his father's place.

And Arjun knew that he had to climb his way to the top.

When Arjun was very worried about not having children, it was Keshtokali who treated him. Arjun has no doubt whatsoever that it is thanks to that treatment that he is now about to become a father.

On his way to the kabiraj, Arjun thinks, does it behove him to feel so very scared?

On hearing the news, Keshtokali Kabiraj lowered his eyes and wrote something for a while. His brow was furrowed, he was deep in thought. When he finally opened his mouth, Arjun wondered if it was his friend speaking or some cross-examining lawyer.

–With this, what's the total in Barnamala?

–What do you mean?

–Do I have to spell it out? Seven years since the building came up. Since then, four maids have died mysterious deaths. All four were pregnant.

–Why are you talking of death?

–Have all the lechers gathered in that one building?

–Are you calling me a lecher?

–You act lecherously. And I won't call you a lech? The maid! Chhi, chhi, Arjun, I take you into my home. You know my whole family . . . My old-fashioned sensibilities are really shocked by this!

–Say what you will. But when you say 'my home', it really hurts. I never dreamt I'd hear you speak this way.

–You've changed a lot, really.

–I am indebted even to the bricks in these walls. I never forget that.

–That chapter closed with my father's death, Arjun. It was Baba who gave you shelter, not I. As soon as you entered college, you moved out and into the hostel. So don't talk to me about debts.

–I did something wrong.

–This is called incest. Incest!

–Your medicine is responsible for this too.

–I've given this medicine to so many, no one has made this kind of a mess with it.

Arjun-babu cannot explain how the sight of Jamuna, day after day, had flooded his heart with such strong desire.

–They come to work driven by desperate hunger. And you lot . . .

–Go ahead, say whatever you want.

–Do what the others have done. Kill the girl, pay off the police.

–Don't say that!

–You're going to be a father after so many years. Such a cause for joy. How much I told you, practise control, strict self-control. You've been given things in life you never even dreamt of! You were childless, even that sorrow is being removed. Just keep control.

Arjun-babu had kept control. At least for a day and a half after Kumkum left, he'd been in strict control. Then, when Jamuna was alone, he . . .

–What's the solution?

–Why have you come to me?

–Isn't there some medicine you can prescribe?

–Me? Do I prescribe medicine for abortions? Your money seems to have really gone to your head!

–I didn't say that.

–Have you ever known me to prescribe such medicine?

–Please forgive me.

Keshtokali, agitated, takes a turn around the room. Gulps down the glass of water on the table. Then wipes the sweat off his forehead, and sits down.

–Listen, Arjun. I don't know if medicine can work in this situation. What to do? Is the girl very frightened?

–She's threatening me.

–Good for her.

–A girl from the slums . . . Her brothers are mastaans . . .

–Who else but a girl from the slums will look for work as a maid? And who doesn't know that such localities are full of mastaans? How often I told you, my brother-in-law has news, reliable news, there's a two-storey house in Bhabanipur for sale. Buy it. A mere twenty-year-old building. Foundation strong enough for four floors, one floor on rent, one floor empty! But you weren't interested.

–Kumkum didn't agree.

–Why would she? Bhabanipur, Kalighat, Chetla—are these places fit for human homes? When you suddenly get money, this is what happens. A new society emerges, and that society needs trendy, fashionable homes. Those buildings are like bazaars. Scandals like this are bound to happen there.

–That's not fair. Such things happen everywhere.

Keshtokali speaks through gritted teeth: Maybe so, Arjun. But whether it's in a slum or a palace, abusing a woman is wrong!

–I agree. I know it's wrong. Now, please tell me what to do.

–When in trouble, run to Keshtokali!

These words lash Arjun like a whip. Yes, he has always, always, got help from Keshtokali whenever he has needed it. But has he repaid him in the same way? Keshtokali had once sent him a needy boy looking for a job, but Arjun didn't give him a place in his office.

–What are you thinking?

–I have made other mistakes too. You sent that boy to me, bhai . . . but one has to keep so many people happy, there are so many requests—

–That you can get away by ignoring one from me.

–What is the boy doing now?

–Not everyone is you. Someone gave him a job as a peon in a bank.

–I am so ashamed. Even so . . .

–Even so! Right. I want some answers.

–What do you want to know?

–Is this woman married?

–Yes, she is.

–Does she have any other children?

–No. She's been married for about a year and a half.

–Does she live with her husband?

–Her husband's factory is shut. He is away looking for a job, visits every now and then.

–Are you the one responsible for her situation?

–Her husband . . . hasn't been for three months . . . also, when Kumkum went away, since then . . .

–What's the woman like?

–Quite cunning and crafty, but not a bad girl. Keeps asking for a job for her husband.

–Understood.

–Tell me what I should do?

–Bring her here.

–Why?

–Hospitals do this all the time, it's not illegal, but your name will be involved. I'll send her to a nursing home I know, they'll do the operation.

–Nursing home?

Keshtokali was a very handsome man, with a face full of character. His lips were thin, and now they twisted into a sharp smile.

–What do you think? That I own the nursing home in another name? Or that I get a commission when I send patients there?

–No, no, not that.

–Listen, try and understand. This is a big responsibility. A cheap nursing home, a sloppy doctor, what if she dies? Such things do happen.

–Great! But the girl's already gone off with one thousand rupees. This will cost some more . . .

–Many thousands can be spent in such cases. You're getting off with just one or two.

–Whatever you say, Keshtokali. Two thousand, three thousand, just handle the scandal somehow. I swear I won't make the same mistake again. I touch your hand and swear, I'll never keep a young maid ever. Never.

–Will you remember?

–I'll remember, I'll remember. Oh, if Kumkum finds out!

–Why should she find out?

–Just saying . . .

Arjun keeps wiping the sweat off his forehead, his nape, his neck. Life! Tempting, seductive life! Until yesterday, Arjunbabu's castle had been safe. Flourishing business, pregnant wife, all his dues rolling in, he could never have imagined that the castle's foundations would crack open like this. And a skeleton tumble out. But that's exactly what happened. This morning, Jamuna . . .

–I'll change my astrologer. He never gave me the slightest indication that something bad was going to happen.

–This attitude is wrong, Arjun! Why such faith in astrologers, anyway? You're the one who made the mistake, and now you're blaming the astrologer?

–Never mind, let it be.

–Stop taking the medicine I gave you. It's a stimulant.

Arjun divides up the blame in his mind. The astrologer is to blame, he'd never once warned him that bad times lay ahead. Keshtokali is to blame, he gave him such a stimulant that his mind was always full of . . . and Jamuna, isn't she to blame too? Why did she have such a body, such ways of walking and talking?

–What are you thinking?

–Does your medicine contain rhino horn?

–This is the age of science, Arjun! Ayurveda today is also based on science. In any case, no one ever reveals what goes into their medicine.

–Let it be, don't tell me.

–Rhino horn! Oh, what a lot of hocus pocus you can believe in!

–Shall I bring her tomorrow?

–Phone me in the morning. I'll only be able to reach the doctor late tonight. I'll talk to him. When you call me in the morning, I'll be able to tell you when to bring her, afternoon or evening. You may even have to take her straight to the nursing home.

–Me?

–Then who? Me?

–I was thinking . . . her brothers . . .

–You think too much.

Arjun just can't accept that the blame lies with him alone. His mind keeps trying to hold other people responsible.

–The police and the government, they're all the same!

–What have the government and the police done now?

–Why, why don't they keep a closer watch on the slums? Why are they full of mastaans? Aren't we citizens too? Don't they have to think about us too? In these last seven or eight years, so many multi-storey apartments have come up there: Barnamala, Sourav, Greenlove, Ashray. All full of decent, genteel folk. Who is thinking of their safety and security?

–Yes! Decent and genteel indeed. Arrey! You're the only ones they're thinking of. Four maids found dead in Barnamala. But was anyone arrested? Don't worry. You can also kill your maid with one hand, pay off the police with the other. Then you'll see, the police are with you.

–I'm not saying that.

–The rich have always gone scot free.

–And what kind of a man is her husband? You know your wife is a live bomb. Then why leave her alone and go off?

–That's enough, Arjun. Don't play the victim here. You're the one who's done wrong. You should be ashamed of your-self. But no. The astrologer, me, the girl, her husband, the police, the government, you're blaming everyone else instead!

–I think I'm losing my mind.

–Here, take this tablet.

–I'll take it now?

–Not now. Take it at home, before sleeping. It'll calm you down.

–It'll make me calm?

–Yes, yes, it will calm you, you'll sleep well.

–You've saved me, bhai!

Keshtokali becomes his sympathetic old friend again. Says gently, It's not good for you to get so agitated. It'll harm only you, no one else. The danger isn't over yet, you know.

–Truly, a huge danger. I'm terrified of the scandal. In Barnamala itself, so many people are envious of me, you have no idea. We do Durga Puja every year. I gift a jewelled nose ring to the goddess. Whatever the price. One thousand rupees donation, and that jewelled nose ring—that's a must. This year Dutta's wife told me, Why a mere nose ring? Why don't you bestow an entire golden crown on Ma!

–That's a good suggestion.

–She didn't mean it nicely! Jealous, they're all jealous of me. If they get word of this scandal, how they'll enjoy themselves at my expense, how much trouble they'll stir up! And Dutta's wife's brother is a journalist. Parakram Sinha. If he gets to hear of this . . .

–No, no, he's a serious journalist. He doesn't write about people's maids.

–Still, I can't help thinking about it.

–Don't think so much. Troubles come, but they also pass. What is needed is discipline, self-control. Practise that.

–I keep thinking of those brothers. You don't know how ferocious they are. Once Kumkum's ladies' club went to distribute clothes to the slum children, and they said, Oh, you've bought sacks full of Joy Bangla castoffs? Take them away, take them away, we can afford to buy these ourselves.

–Well, you flaunt your fancy cars and houses in front of them. No wonder they're ferocious.

–Mrs Desai is mad. Apparently one day she said something to the boy who works for her, and within minutes ten or twelve women ambushed her husband on the street.

–Don't think of all that. The girl will have her operation, she'll leave the next day. Or give her some more money and send her packing.

–That I will anyway. What a girl, says she knows where I stash my money in the house.

–What's her salary?

–Not sure. Maybe a hundred rupees. Anything less and they won't touch a dirty dish. It's their world now, after all. That house has no TV?—no, won't work there. Won't drink water unless it's from the fridge. Four sets of clothes a year . . .

–Bound to happen. Even here the demands have gone up, although not that much. And in truth how can we protest? The prices have skyrocketed! Everything is so expensive. Still, ours is a middle-class neighbourhood. A little less harsh.

–Your good fortune, bhai! Boudi cooks and serves herself, I know.

–And thus suffers perennially from acidity! It's a bit of a mania with her. She won't let go of the cooking. Between puja, cooking, eating at odd hours, no wonder she suffers from heartburn.

–I'd better be going, bhai. Have to visit my wife. Have dinner there.

–See you soon.

–Got married at twenty-five. Got pregnant at thirty-five! Wonderful, great news. But you have no idea how clingy she's become! She phones every day, I have to visit her, take her flowers when I go!

–It's only natural, eh?

–Not natural at all. The way Kumkum's behaving these days is absolutely not natural. Did Boudi ever act like this, tell me?

–Our case is different. An old-fashioned household. We never saw our wives except at night. Got married young. Had children young. See, you and I, we're both forty-four. My oldest daughter is twenty-two, I've got her married already. And just the other day I became a grandfather. As you know, my sons are twins. Both have done their B.Com, they're now studying CA. They're also past twenty. And the younger daughter's seventeen.

–Boudi never acted so silly, did she?

–Arrey! Your Boudi is the eldest daughter-in-law of a large household. Plus she had all her children at her father's house. There's been none of that coy-clingy stuff in our family. You were here, then—did you ever set eyes on my sisters? Things were very strict.

36

–This clingy behaviour of Kumkum's is not at all normal. Did you know, for the past ten years she's called me a eunuch?

–That makes me so sad. Husband and wife . . . there should be respect, devotion.

–Every chance she gets, she tells me I have no culture, I only know money.

–That's not good. But you'll see, once she has a child, she'll change. Something was missing inside her. That's why she used to say all this.

–She keeps cooking all that exotic rubbish for you—of course you'll support her!

–All the stuff I never get to eat here, that's what your wife . . . and she cooks well too.

–Yes, yes. She cooks Spanish meat curry out of a book. Mexican mishmash. I, on the other hand, like kalai dal, alu-posto, spicy fish curry . . . yet I can't remember when I last ate all that.

–Just wait till your Boudi hears you haven't . . . Oof! I eat all that stuff all day! And then go to your house for a change of taste! Here, in our household, she's the one in charge, after all. As soon as it's summer, it's neem-begun, raw-mango curry. Then in the monsoons, the mishmash of kochu greens.

–Oh, stop, stop! Drumsticks, neem leaves, kochu greens—these are banned from our home. Apparently, they're too awful to be eaten.

–Convent-educated mother-in-law, convent-educated wife. You want all that, and you also want your drumsticks! Is it possible to have it all?

–I'm off. If I don't buy the flowers, she'll burst into tears. These days she cries at every little thing. The way you're cloying and clinging to me today, pouting and asking for treats as if you're a seventeen-year-old! If you had paid me even a quarter of a quarter of this attention over the past ten years, would I have been in this state today?

–How bad a state are you in, really?! In a bit of a fix today, but you'll come out of it.

–I mean, Kumkum has an MA in philosophy. She's thirty-five. And eight months pregnant. Her latest whim is to have a huge anniversary celebration at her parents'. Does that make any sense?

–Marriage . . . motherhood . . . Indian tradition.

–Rubbish!

*

Arjun-babu leaves in a lighter frame of mind. No, the mood he'd been in when he arrived, that mood has lifted. Keshtokali was right. The operation will be done in secret, in the nursing home, no one will know. And then, if need be, he'll pay Jamuna some more money and send her away.

He won't see Jamuna again; just the thought of it makes him sad. But what else can he do? Judge-sahib's short fat daughter Kumkum, he'll have to spend the rest of his life looking at her.

Flowers, he must buy flowers! To play the love-struck husband at this age was rather difficult. But the flowers are a must.

Flowers, flowers! Who'll buy these?
Bela – malati – champa – juthi
Intoxicating the swarm of bees!

Why has this old song suddenly entered his head? Because he's feeling lighter?

He stops the car and buys a bouquet of roses. How will Jamuna look with one of these roses in her hair? And if she pairs it with a yellow nylon sari? No, Arjun-babu won't think of Jamuna any more. That he's still thinking of her right now, this is because of that Keshtokali's medicine. It's after taking that medicine that . . .

Stop it! Mind, control yourself!

Arjun arrives at Harbour Apartments on Camac Street.

FIVE

The lift swoops him up to the eighth floor. To his father-in-law's flat. Every door bears a brass knocker shaped like a Tibetan tiger-lion-demon-deity head. The doorbell too has a melodious tone. As if someone is playing the piano.

Bhaswati opens the door. Bhaswati is Arjun's sole brother-in-law's wife. She has a long, horsey face, large teeth.

But Bhaswati is a ladies' bridge champion. A regular bridge columnist for an English daily, no mean feat. She's also the Public Relations Officer in some company or other.

Today, she gives him a mischievous smile.

–Why are you so late?

–Am I very?

–Your wife's boiling with rage.

–How come you're here?

–Because we're eating here too! Kumkum phoned, and following her orders, I've brought tandoori chicken from Feroze. It's amazing, you'll see!

Bhaswati must be thirty-eight. Red Dhakai sari, red blouse, gold earrings as large as coachwheels, a huge sindoor bindi.

–I've dressed up like a new bride!

–So I see!

Arjun thinks to himself, The hotel you go to with Randhawa is where I take my clients for a drink. Seen you there four days in a row. The same four days when you were apparently away on an office tour. You can dangle those earrings all you want, but you can't bring Arjun Chakrabarty under your spell, so don't even try.

The sitting room is huge. His father-in-law'd been a Supreme Court judge. The interior has been designed by a professional firm. As a result, the chairs are weird, the table is weird, and on the curtains angry dragons breathe fire. Even a brass idol of the lion-mounted goddess Durga, behind a glass screen on the wall, has not been spared from serving as decor.

The chairs look as if they were made on Mars. Twisted and bent.

Kumkum is sitting in one such chair. A white printed sari, white blouse, pearls at her neck, pearls in her hair. Arjun steps forward. Holds out the bouquet.

What does Kumkum want? She shows no interest in the bouquet. He stands there, clutching it. Buries his face in the flowers, takes a deep breath and says, Darling! Darling!

Bhaswati says, Take the flowers.

–You take them, Boudi. Darling! Come sit near me. You're so late! I'm so tired, worrying about you.

–Why do you worry so much?

–Ba! Won't I worry about you?

–But you know, darling, that I have a lot of work.

At this juncture, Head of the Household, retired Judge-sahib, opines: No matter how busy you are, you must make time for my Mimi-moppet.

At one time, his convent-educated mother-in-law had been an energetic horse rider and keen singer of 'Netaji zindabad!'–type patriotic songs. She was also a regular party hostess in Delhi as well as an adept networker. Many say that it was only due to her efforts that her husband rose to become a Supreme Court judge.

Now, her hair is trimmed short. And, even at sixty-two, she regularly she visits the salon for beauty treatments. A solid, toned body. Every morning, the tall Judge-sahib and his short Judge-missus take to the streets for their daily run.

How a lady like this had been named Runujhunu, Arjun simply cannot fathom.

His mother-in-law always orates, never converses. As if she's at the United Nations, lecturing on Africa. In just such a tone she now says: Becoming a mother for the first time at thirty-five is a very serious matter. We cannot imagine what her body is going through. But that her mind doesn't endure any tension, we can make sure of that. Men are so oblivious to women! This can only happen in India.

The in-laws had been on a month-long conducted tour of Europe and America. They are thus qualified to hold forth on a comparative study between foreign men and Indian men.

Judge-sahib removes his cheroot to say, He's busy, he's busy. Arjun doesn't do a nine-to-five job. He has a lot of work. Also, becoming a father for the first time at the age of forty-four has its own tensions, don't forget that.

While this exchange is in progress, Arjun sits there holding Kumkum's hand. Kumkum's head rests on his shoulder.

Ah, such faith she has in him, she's so at peace! With such a Kumkum in his life, how could Arjun go running after Jamuna?

The mind within the mind now does its magic. And starts an argument between Sanatan Pushilal and Arjun Chakravarty. Arjun knows, these people can never imagine that he was born Sanatan Pushilal, that he too is twice-born. If those born from an egg are twice-born—once as an egg, and once again as a sentient being—then Arjun is definitely twice-born as well. Lizards, crocodiles, turtles, most snakes (some snakes can birth babies directly—how amazing!), birds, he is twice-born like all of them. Even pearls are twice-born. First the oyster, then the pearl.

Changing one's name by affidavit alone does not make one twice-born. Twice-born means those who are born again, re-born. Like a brahmin is born again through his sacred-thread ceremony. People can change their names for many reasons, and why shouldn't they? They can do so even if they don't like the name they already have. The father is 'Pond', they become 'Ocean'. Inheritance, business, whimsy, there are so many reasons why people change their names.

Does a new name make someone a twice-born?

Arjun doesn't know. He doesn't.

He is definitely twice-born, born twice over, he doesn't even remember Sanatan Pushilal any more.

Sanatan Pushilal would like to say, When you have a wife, chasing another woman . . . is not right.

Arjun Chakravarty doesn't bother to reply. Continues to stroke Kumkum's forehead. A strange smile on his lips.

Sanatan, oh Sanatan, don't hold me back! I know I've erred, I also know that I won't err again.

Runujhunu, pacing up and down, says, Arjun, Arjun. Can't you tell that Kumkum isn't as strong as I am. I had two children, but there were no problems. It's not like their father was with me all the time either.

–She's in your care. What could be more reassuring?

–Husbands have a responsibility too. Can you imagine? When Bhaskar was born, his father was so busy with that famous Elba Bank fraud case, yet he came to the nursing home every day.

The father-in-law clears his throat. To soothe his wife, he says, My dear! We were different. We were dreaming of Independence, then.

What do you mean? Bhaswati says, How often have we heard that your son and daughter were born after Independence?!

Runujhunu smiles. Bhaskar is a day older than our Independence, she proudly declares, He was born on 14 August. Kumkum, of course, came after.

Bhaswati eyes her askance. Well, now I know the truth. All this while I thought that Bhaskar and I were the same age.

We got his age lowered by affidavit, Runujhunu continues without changing her tone, Keeping his job applications in mind. We thought you knew.

Never mind all that, the father-in-law says, Arjun!

Arjun starts. Yes?

–What have you thought about the doctor?

–Doctor! Keshtokali will—

Arjun bites his tongue, stops himself. Careful, Arjun, be careful. The doctor Keshtokali is fixing is for Jamuna. In secret.

–Keshtokali? You mean that kabiraj of yours?

–No, no, Keshtokali was recommending Dr Choudhury, he's very famous. He may be a kabiraj, but he keeps himself informed . . .

Kumkum giggles like a little girl.

–What's wrong with you today? If I'm not with you, you forget everything!

–What did I forget?

–Who is this Dr Choudhury? For the past four months, it's Dr Ray who's been looking after me!

Acting, one must keep acting. Or they'll find out everything.

–Of course, Dr Ray! Such arguments over that bridge matter today, so many explanations over and over, I just can't take it any more. They'll drive me crazy.

These days his father-in-law gets all his news from the newspapers, and for some reason seems to think he knows much more about the news than the newspapers print. He nods.

–The engineers are giving trouble, eh?

That wasn't the problem. But Arjun will say yes for now. It's best that way.

–You have no idea!

–If government engineers throw a spanner in the works like this, I'm telling you, Arjun—Runu, you should hear this— if doctors, engineers start acting up, our hard-won Independence will be ruined!

Kumkum protests sweetly, Bapi!

–No, no, we shouldn't be discussing work matters in front of you, Mimi-moppet.

Arjun says, I have absolutely no intention of bringing in another doctor. How could I? Dr Ray is recommended by you two, after all. You are all there for her, I have no one, no family. I am totally dependent on you.

Bhaswati says, That's true.

Kumkum asks, Boudi, when you had your Bibi, were you this nervous?

Bhaswati neighs with laughter.

–Kumkum, working women are never nervous. And Dr Ray is my uncle, don't forget! I wasn't scared at all.

–Your mother, of course . . .

–My mother was very tough. At home we used to call her 'Soldier'. Baba called her 'Captain'.

Arjun thinks, You're no less a lady captain yourself, Bhaswati. You're practically soaring, flying high for quite a while now, I know all about it.

Kumkum says, When I'm not at home, you get everything so muddled up.

His mind says, Oof, my little coy cuckoo! How much time did you spend at home, and how much did you spend on me? You were always rushing about, obsessed with 'culture'.

His mouth says, You are my . . .

His father-in-law says, Drinks, Arjun? Bhaskar?

And Bhaskar screams, Pregnant! Pregnant!

Arjun, terrified, yells, Who? Who?

Bhaskar waves *The Statesman* at him, The crossword, I say, the crossword! I was stuck for this one word. But why're you so startled? Mimi's been expecting for months!

His father-in-law says, Enough.

His mother-in-law says, Just one round, that's all.

–Scotch on the rocks?

–Why not.

–Gin and lime for me!

–Bhaswati, gin. Runu, you?

His mother-in-law says in a grim voice, Brandy.

–Mimi-moppet?

–Jeera-pani, Bapi.

–Then have a Rimzim.

A gulp or two of the Scotch, and Arjun feels much better. When Bhaskar yelled 'pregnant', he'd been scared out of his wits.

Bhaswati sips at her gin and lime.

Runujhunu drinks her brandy.

Kumkum touches her lips to her Rimzim, and watches him like a cat.

Bhaskar is again lost in his crossword.

His father-in-law says, Bhaskar, if you want to do the crossword, keep *The Telegraph*.

–I do. I've done that one already. Wait, this word . . .

Kumkum says lovingly, Don't be late with dinner, Ma. He has to go home.

Bhaswati says, So do we.

–You're just here, on Park Street. Think how far he has to go.

Bhaswati says, I want to get home early today. What an uproar in No. 12!

–What happened?

–The ayah stole everything and fled! Tell me, if our maids-ayahs-houseboys are going to keep cleaning us out, what's the point of paying so much for a security service? This is the third time this year.

His mother-in-law says, No one stays at home. Everything left lying around . . .

Bhaskar says, Work is work, Ma! How many are as fortunate as you? The same old cook, the same old maid!

–Yes, we're truly lucky.

Kumkum says, We are too.

Bhaswati says, All part-timers?

–Yes, yes. Mohini does the cooking and goes away. Oh, listen dear, I hope Mohini is doing everything properly?

–Yes, she is.

–You'll of course eat whatever's put in front of you. Remember how I'd cook a new dish every day?

His mind says, New dish my foot. Something out of a book, and that too always inedible.

His mouth says, Can anyone ever cook like you?

–That's why I left instructions, make this today, that tomorrow. Is Bahadur doing the dusting properly?

–Yes, very well.

–Nothing should get broken.

–No, no, I keep an eye on things.

–I don't have to check on Jamuna, of course.

–You mean that Brigitte Bardot?

–The things you say, Boudi! Jamuna is excellent! Washes clothes so well, irons beautifully, and how carefully she mops that huge flat! Shampoos my hair, combs my hair for me.

–She's a beauty, whatever you say.

–How she adores her husband! Although he's unemployed, and also has a terrible temper.

Runujhunu says sternly, This is why there's no future for the women of this country. Their husbands don't work, only show their tempers. The wives slave to feed them, but the men feel no shame. Not man enough to put food on the table. Breed swarms of children.

Kumkum bursts out laughing.

–Ma! Jamuna has no children yet. She's not been married for long. Had a regular love marriage. If you met her, you'd see.

–Why won't I see? I've seen a lot. But you, Mimi. You must maintain some distance. Giving her the same clothes that you wear, that is how they get spoilt.

–But I don't like to see them come to work in shabby clothes. If our servants are not well dressed, our prestige suffers. It doesn't look good.

Bhaswati gives a twisted smile. I call your Jamuna Brigitte Bardot. Can she do some modelling?

Kumkum may be spoilt and pampered, but her brain is not that sharp, her mind simple.

–Why should she do modelling? She's so happy working for me. She tells me, I work in so many houses, but no one is as warm hearted as you, Boudi!

–Careful! So much trust is not a good thing.

–No, Boudi. She's different. She calls Ma and Baba Dadu and Didima. She calls you two Mama and Mami.

–And what does she call your husband?

Arjun was growing more and more restless.

–Achcha, can't we stop discussing Jamuna? Do you both have nothing else to talk about?

Kumkum says, You don't know what luck it is to find a trustworthy, decent worker. She even did a puja for me, unasked. It wasn't part of her job!

Brandy has mellowed the mother-in-law.

–Mimi has always been like this. Ayah-gardener-bearer, she loved them all. She'd say, On my birthday, you must give them new clothes too.

Bhaswati says, All this talk is making it late, Ma. Let's eat.

The father-in-law suddenly asks, What's the security service like in Barnamala? Is it good?

–Seems to be.

The mother-in-law gets up and walks off. In this flat, the dining room is separate from the living room. Judge-sahib's wife has lived her life in government houses. Here, too, she maintains the old ways as far as possible.

The dining room is also large. Everyone sits at the table. Kumkum says, Ei, eat properly.

–I am.

–Boudi brought the tandoori. Also the saffron pulao, the steamed prawns . . .

–Can one eat so much?!

–I don't know why, but today I felt like eating all my favourite dishes. Although that's not entirely possible, because these days what I crave most is pineapples. Chilled pineapple with chilled cream. Fabulous!

–Pineapple? You're eating pineapple?

–Why? Shouldn't I?

–Keshtokali says—

–Never mind all that. The doctor's told me I can eat whatever I want.

The father-in-law spears a piece of prawn with his fork and says, Arjun! Your friend may be a good kabiraj, but that doesn't mean he knows everything.

Bhaskar says, That stuff is all hocus pocus!

Kumkum says, Eesh! Do you know everything?

Bhaswati says, To each his own.

The dining table is a rotating one. You help yourself from one dish, then turn the table so it moves to the next person. The funny thing is, right in the centre is another gleaming, independently rotating wooden piece. You turn it, and the dish you want is before you.

At the end of the meal, an onion pudding is served. Arjun cannot fathom why anyone would want a pudding made of onions.

–Well, Arjun-babu?

–Yes, Bhaswati?

–What about that matter?

–Matter? What matter?

Don't scare me like this, don't scare me you lot. I need peace, mental calm, undisturbed tranquillity. No, Keshtokali's medicine won't do. I will have to take the stress-busting tablet in my pocket. Having taken it for a few days, Arjun has understood its special powers. Sends you flying right into the sky.

–Why is everything startling you so?

–Had a very bad day.

Bhaskar softened a bit. Said, Bhaswati was talking about your wedding anniversary.

–Fine, Kumkum wants it, it'll be done.

–Don't you want it?

–If Kumkum wants it, I want it as well.

The mother-in-law looks across at Bhaswati with pride. See, see how devoted my son-in-law is to my daughter. Is your husband like that?

Bhaskar is a chartered accountant. He does some calculations in his head, then says, I have a proposal. Everyone must say yes.

Bhaswati says, Why should we?

–First hear me out.

–Go on, Dada. I'm listening.

–Not just Mimi and Arjun. Every year for Baba–Ma's anniversary, we put a congratulatory insert in *The Statesman*. Baba–Ma–Mimi–your brother, for our anniversary we put out a 'best wishes' announcement. This year I'm about to be an uncle. Such auspicious news. This year, let's have a party for Mimi's anniversary, for Baba–Ma's anniversary and for ours as well. Why not?

Bhaswati says, I'm only too happy. But—

–What?

–Ma must wear a Benarasi saree!

–I will.

The words 'I will' were spoken in the tone one might use to say 'I will die for my country'.

Bhaskar says, No, no, this is our duty. Couples who are happily married, those marriages should be celebrated. Especially nowadays, when . . .

Bhaswati, licking her dessert spoon, says, When?

–When so many marriages are breaking up.

–Can one tell from the outside?

–Only after spending many years together.

53

Arjun wants to burst out laughing. How long has Keshto-kali been married? They are happy too. That Mohini, their cook, if she is to be believed, and if she is truly sixty years old, then for the past fifty years she's been quarrelling with her husband and saying, 'Why doesn't this good-for-nothing die!' Their anniversary definitely needs to be celebrated, they just don't know it.

Kumkum suddenly says, Ma! Remember Mira Bhargava? You got so angry at first, but then you ended up going, I still remember.

–I got angry because there was good reason to be angry. I went because it was a social obligation.

–Who's Mira Bhargava?

–Oh, Boudi! It was ages ago. In Delhi. Mira wanted to marry someone . . . I think he was a Muslim. You won't believe it, she apparently got cholera one night and then by daybreak it was all over—the body burnt to ash. They'd murdered her for sure, poison or something, you know? What a shameful scandal it was!

Judge-sahib says, Mimi! There was no case, nothing, it's not right to call it murder. Think carefully before you say such things.

–You can say what you like. And just a few days after, the Bhargavas celebrated their anniversary in such a fancy way! Ma was so angry.

Arjun softly says, Let it be.

–Yes, let's talk about us. I don't care how I'll look, I'm going to wear a new Benarasi.

Bhaswati says, We'll decorate your husband's car with flowers like a groom's car, hire a shehnai player to pay wedding tunes.

Bhaskar says, Yes, yes, let's be happy.

For some reason Arjun also keeps thinking, yes, let's be happy, happy.

Kumkum says, Ei! What are you doing tomorrow?

He almost says, Tomorrow I'm taking Jamuna to the nursing home. Because, Kumkum, she is pregnant with my child. It's vital that I sort out this mess.

–Ei! Say something!

–Tomorrow? Tomorrow I have a meeting marathon. I also have to visit the site. Would you believe it? We've been buying wood from the Opel Company, no less. But they've dumped us with rubbish stocks?

–You won't come tomorrow?

–I'll try.

After washing their hands, they all go back to the sitting room.

The mother-in-law says, Mimi! It's time to go to bed now. You must maintain your timings.

–I was just going. Ei!

–Yes?

–You'd better start thinking of a new home.

–Why?

–There's a child coming. Will that small flat be enough? After all, he's going to grow.

Kumkum! Kumkum! Isn't there space for a child in that 2,500-square-foot flat? If one needs 5,000 square feet per child, then how much space will ever be enough? What are you saying?

–You want a bigger flat?

–Not a flat. I want a house, a house.

Oh, my dear heart! You delight me so. Is a house a kitten or a kite, that one can just buy it in a shop to make one's wife happy? You're a parent now, be pure of mind, think of god. If you have good thoughts, your child will be good. Or else he'll be like me . . .

–Let's see.

–Plus that area's awful.

That stings Bhaskar, stings Bhaswati too. Bhaskar and Kumkum may be each other's only siblings. But Kumkum's flat is much larger than theirs. Theirs is only 2,200 square feet. They have just one car, and Bhaswati has to use the office car to and from work. While Kumkum alone has two cars, and contractor Arjun, if he so wants, can have ten at his disposal. For Kumkum's birthday, they may gift her a sari worth three hundred rupees, but Kumkum gives them both, and their child, nothing worth less than a thousand. Same for the Pujas. And then she acts all coy and cute, says, I'm your poor sister, I've given whatever little I could.

For all these reasons Bhaskar and Bhaswati have a lot of envy in their hearts, a lot. Why do they have so much and why don't we is the cause of much marital strife.

But to so casually ask for a new house, to leave the locality itself?

Bhaskar asks, Why is that locality so awful, Mimi? This world belongs to Arjun and his ilk. In a trice Barnamala after Barnamala will rise, the slums will recede, then vanish. Then that same locality will be a posh locality.

The mother-in-law says, Mimi. Stop this childishness. You may want an exclusive neighbourhood but will you find a house there, or even a plot of land? Apart from Loudon, Camac, Harrington, Alipore, where else are the refined neighbourhoods in Kolkata?

Bhaswati perhaps suddenly remembers that Arjun often sees her at the hotel. With Randhawa. No, it's not a good idea to offend him.

She puts on her best Public Relations Officer voice and says, You want to leave that neighbourhood. But if you do, will you find domestic help? Think of what Ma has said. If you want a substantial piece of land for a house, then you'll have to go far off, to Salt Lake or near the Bypass.

Judge-sahib keeps saying, True, true.

What a scoundrel the old man is! Which of them is right? The daughter's caprice? His wife's barbs? Or Bhaswati's peace-keeping efforts?

Oof, just let me go! I want to go home. I want to sit in the car and take my tablet. Take my Ayurveda too, take my milk and my tobacco. And then home, home, home sweet home! Where will I find a home as lovely. I want to go home. Lie down in my cool room, on my cool sheets, read a book and slowly . . .

–Kumkum, don't stress yourself with all this. We all want you to be tension free and happy. Now I should go.

–I really want to come back home for a day.

–Don't be childish. Off you go, go to sleep like a good girl.

Arjun gets up to leave. Bhaskar and Bhaswati also start saying their goodbyes.

Suddenly Judge-sahib says, Drive carefully, Arjun, you seemed quite agitated today.

–Yes, I will.

Why wouldn't I be agitated? This home of yours, the things you talk about! The father-in-law pours a drink for his own wife, for his son's wife too. As if this land is a foreign land, and you're all foreigners. If Arjun wishes, he can buy you and your son right now. Buy a house too in this very neighbourhood. He doesn't; he doesn't want to draw attention to himself. Too much greed can sink everything you've achieved. Can he afford to forget all that?

In the car, he swallows both the tablet and the Kabiraji medicine. Happiness, happiness, suddenly Arjun is awash in happiness. How happy he feels! Why is that?

SIX

He enters the flat with his key, shuts the door. Runs to the bathroom. Doesn't run as much as float. Is this because of the tablet or the Kabiraj's medicine?

Bahadur has laid out his pyjamas, towel, vest in the bathroom. In this bathroom, everything from the bathtub to the shower is blue.

Blue his room, walls, carpet, curtains.

In the green room, everything is green. In the dining room, everything is orange. The room kept aside for guests is a–l–l pink.

It's into this pink room, through the pink bathroom, that Jamuna used to come. Jamuna! Jamuna! And on that soft pink carpet she would lay down her body and rest. That first time she'd fought him off, hit him hard, it's true, but who can resist Arjun? A superman, he is! Thanks to the Kabiraji medicine, his manhood has awakened, roaring like a lion . . .

Oh, a poem is coming to him unbidden, a poem! What happiness the tablet brings, Keshtokali! You've never tried it, you'll never know. You'll never know either what heavenly bliss it is to take a dip in the Jamuna, you damned moralistic Keshtokali! Ah Jamuney, are you the same Jamuney? All those names you called me this morning—old lech, maggot, devil? Say them again, go on, say them, I'm not angry with you any more.

There is a security guard outside. From nine at night to early morning, he patrols the corridors.

There is really no need to check the whole flat. Nevertheless, Arjun is often overcome by the sudden need to do so.

A home like this, a beautiful home like this, couldn't a little boy crawl around in it? Arjun puts on his pyjamas and vest without bothering to towel himself totally dry, and comes out of the bathroom. Ah! Stars bursting in his head, shining stars. My son! Be a boy. Don't be born a girl, for god's sake. Be a boy!

Won't you have room enough to crawl about? Let's see if I can crawl a little. This is not me crawling, it's the tablet. Still, what fun! I will kiss you. Kiss kiss kus kus!

In the blue room, on the blue carpet, A-babu starts to crawl. This is quite the football field, eh! If you crawl through all three rooms, you'll be exhausted! How big the green room carpet is, how b–i–g! Crawl, let me crawl . . . Let me crawl into the pink room now.

The guest room. Should he be a guest in his own home tonight? What if he sleeps on the pink bed? And why shouldn't he? He is the monarch of his own empire.

But as soon as he sees the pink bedcover, why does he think dirty thoughts? What is this you've done, Keshtokali? What did you feed me, that I'm thinking dirty thoughts all the time?

No more crawling. Now I'll get up, now I'll walk—but at the far corner of the pink carpet, who is that fast asleep, the edge of her yellow sari spread under her?

Hundreds of drums begin to beat in his blood. Hundreds. Jamuna, Jamuna, you've come? You're the one I was longing for. Is this telepathy? Did my mind reach out to yours, and so you used your key and came in through the bathroom door?

Clever girl, clever girl, you know that the flat is empty after five. No Mohini, no Bahadur, no one.

Tomorrow itself I'll take you via Keshtokali to the nursing home. I'll go, yes I'll go, to the nursing home I'll go! But just for tonight, naughty girl, sweet girl! Kiss kiss kus kus, won't you wake up? Even when I kiss your two eyes, won't you wake up?

Moving closer, trying to kiss her, suddenly Arjun's head is full of Bhopal gas. Something bursts in his brain, the stars blow away.

Jamuna is dead!

–Jamuna! Ei, Jamuna!

He feels her heart, her pulse. Froth at the edge of her mouth, tears at the corner of her eyes.

–N–o–o–o–o . . . no!

Arjun babu crumples to the ground. The hand still so soft, but Jamuna's dead?

Saffron pulao, tandoori chicken, prawns, onion pudding, they all rise up in revolt.

Bathroom! Bathroom! And then vomit everywhere. He'll have to clean it up.

He turns on the shower, tries to calm down. Then he starts to think.

Alas, he is not to know that Jamuna had indeed gone to Lame Doctor. High on ganja, charas, cocaine and whatnot, Lame Doctor thought he was giving her one thing but it was something else entirely.

He is not to know that Jamuna, twirling her keys, told Johnny and Tala, I'll take the medicine and go there to rest, OK? Mohini, Bahadur, they all know me, besides the flat will be empty. Where else can I get such comfort?

If the medicine works, she has to use the bathroom a lot. That will be easier in the flat too.

He is not to know that as soon as she took the medicine, Jamuna was overcome, that she slowly slid to the ground, that there was an unbearable pain in her chest yet her throat could emit no sound.

Arjun-babu calms down and emerges from the bathroom. It is late now, late at night. Should he inform the police?

No, no police.

Should he call the security guard?

No, not another soul. Nobody must be told. Whoever you tell will blackmail you.

Does he ever reveal the secret mysteries of his contractor methods? Whoever knows, knows.

Arjun-babu has learnt a lot from reading books. The books that have taught him are all kept in his bedroom. Walk into his room, and you'll see rows of paperbacks by John MacDonald, James Hadley Chase, Lawrence Sanders, Ed McBain and many more such.

The library in the sitting room had been set up by the interior-decorator firm. They are the ones who set up libraries in the homes of the nouveau riche.

Junk, really.

The books are not arranged by subject. They're just heaped together. Some lie bent on their side, some shelfs are half empty.

So that one glance is enough to tell that this is a person who really reads. These books are not just home decor. Every subject under the sun is here.

Philosophy, fiction, absurd theatre, oceanology, short stories, space research, international revolutionaries' biographies, ornithology, Black protest literature, shikaar tales, histories of Third World revolutions, poetry, travel—whatever you want.

But will those books tell him how Jamuna died?

Murder?

Suicide?

Accident?

No, no book holds the answer.

West Bengal is an absolutely atrocious place. Crime is endless, but is there anybody to write about it? Then are the words spoken by the hero in that Thompson novel true, that all humans contain the will to commit murder but not all of them use it?

Anyway, let it go, no point thinking about all that. He is the one in grave danger now.

Alas, it's so hard to keep oneself safe, secure. So impossible.

Where does he stand right now?

Jamuna works in other flats in the building, as she does in his. She spends more hours here, stays a longer time.

Kumkum left for her parents' house, and Jamuna and he . . . he and Jamuna . . . Mohini knows. Bahadur knows too.

The guard definitely knows.

Since Arjun did not think of them as human beings, he hadn't felt scared, hadn't felt any shame. But now, they're the ones he's thinking about.

He won't go to the police. Why should he? If he was the one who had killed her, then he would have spoken to the police, paid them off, turned the story around. Barnamala has seen such cases before.

Why should he?

He had wanted to spend a lot of money and take her to the nursing home to relieve her of her burden.

Why don't the Jamunas ever trust the Arjun-babus? He was responsible for her pregnancy, not for her death—how can he explain this?

A bad time, such a bad time!

Kumkum, thirty-five years old and eight months pregnant, is insisting on an anniversary celebration.

You keep telling me, You have no culture. And what you want to do, where's the good taste in that? Every year, you get to see the good wishes announcement in *The Statesman*. Isn't that enough? It's all so fake! Putting a notice in the papers to let us know you're happy!

A bad time, such a bad time!

He'd greased the right palms for the Konka Bridge contract, the tender was all but his—and at such a moment, what have you gone and done, Jamuna?

If this gets out, it's the end.

The palms he's greased belong to one of Kumkum's uncles. What a bold pronouncement he made! If I can give it to a relative, I won't give it to anyone else. I believe in family unity!

It'll all turn to shit. Oh my beautifully tended orchard! Sucked dry, my beautiful orchard.

Got to dance to his tune if he wants a way out.

Only one way out.

He needs to move Jamuna out of his flat. At once. Where else did Jamuna work? In which homes?

A sudden bolt of lightning in his brain. Half-visible, half-invisible, an electric vine blazes in his head, fills it with light.

Arrey! Jamuna also worked in Ila Desai's house! And their guest-bathroom door is bang opposite his own!

Once he and Kumkum had lost their keys like fools, oh, what a calamity! One of their close friends, a senior police officer had said, You call this a calamity!

–Well, isn't it?

–Arrey, Abdul has a doctorate in key making. I'll get him to make another.

–Is he in jail?

–What's that to you?

Then, presenting him with a bunch of master keys on some anniversary or birthday, his friend had said, Now don't you turn into a thief or burglar, OK?

Let the night deepen, let it strike one. Ila Desai is mentally unstable. Desai-saheb spends all day tending to her. At night, they both take sleeping pills . . .

There, found a way out.

Why am I feeling hungry?

Because I threw up everything?

Is this hunger or lust? That too is a kind of hunger, after all. In a hungry world, there are so many different kinds of hunger.

Arjun-babu walks to the dining room and opens the fridge. Bread, butter, cheese, it's enough.

He gobbles the food, gulps water. The body needs strength, stamina. So much work to do, so much. Can't afford to be weak now.

Having eaten his fill, a stronger Arjun goes from room to room, switching off the lights. Only the no-power coloured lights are left on. The rooms all look ghostly now.

Now, to work. Retrieve the master key from the locker behind the bookshelf. Slowly, slowly, open the pink-bathroom door. Take a good look around. Yes, all is peaceful, silent, calm.

Other than the sweepers, no one comes this way, no one could be bothered to.

Tiptoe to No. 7, unlock the bathroom door.

Now get the job done quick.

But he feels scared to touch Jamuna, can't bring himself to. At the corner of her mouth, froth or drool. He wipes it away roughly with the corner of her sari. That very same yellow sari!

Tears at the edge of her eyes, tears! Oh, how she must have wept, how she must have suffered, the poor girl! Why did I not drench her in my tears . . . Mind, calm yourself! There's no salvation for him who in his darkest hour starts to think of a song.

Mind! You're not a free bird. You inhabit Arjun-babu's body. Now you must understand—

Arjun-babu has not committed murder but he can be accused of it any moment. If word gets out?

Shame, scandal, disgrace.

Every flat in every building in Barnamala will erupt in cheers.

Just the other day, Lalwani said, Arjun-babu! Typical Bengali babu! Sinking sinking drinking water, eh? The ones who look simple on the outside, they're the ones who on the inside . . .

Lifting Jamuna almost knocks the breath out of him. Are the dead so heavy? The living Jamuna had been like a wave, bird, gazelle. Ah! Again, he's lapsing into poetry!

He hefts her up. Her mouth gives off the sharp smell of poison. What did you take, what killed you, Jamuna? Did you commit suicide? Or was it some crack pill from a quack doctor that did you in?

Tiptoe, tiptoe, across the short corridor, then lower her body into the dry, unused bathtub. Desai, Desai, I have no quarrel with you. Your wife is crazy, your daughter and son-in-law are dead, your son lives in Bombay—you have really suffered.

On top of all this, I have added the burden of Jamuna's dead body. Forgive me. But when bad times begin, best to save your own skin.

He shuts Desai's bathroom door. The service to this flat is different from the others. Desai himself checks and oils every lock, nut, bolt and screw. Earlier he would get the house painted as often as he could.

Now get back to your own flat, Arjun, shut the door. Too late he remembers that he's left his fingerprints all over Desai's bathroom door. Forgot to wipe them off.

Eesh! The murderers in Dick Lebridge's books never slip up like this. As soon as they've killed, they wipe their prints clean.

Forget it, their case is different. They're killers. Arjun-babu is not living in Monte Carlo or Marseilles or Mexico or Chicago, and unlike Dick Lebridge's murderers he does not choke them to death with a wire noose or a nylon stocking or curtain rope. He isn't meant to remember to wipe away his prints.

The door is shut. Arjun-babu switches on the light. How can he know where Jamuna sat, or what she did? Which signs should he erase? Drool from her mouth has fallen onto the pink carpet. Is it easy to clean the stain off a carpet? He doesn't even know how it's done.

Ting tong, ting tong!

The doorbell.

His heart pole-vaults and crashes to the floor. Who rings the bell so late at night? Jamuna's thug brothers? Her husband? How could they come upstairs? He looks through the peephole.

The security guard's face.

He opens the door.

–What do you want so late at night?

–I saw the light go on, then off. You came home so long ago. I just wondered if anyone else had entered . . .

–Anyone else?

–A thief . . .

No, no thief or thug. It was Jamuna who had come. To die. But you don't know this.

–It's me, just me, there's no one else.

–All right, then. Salaam, saheb.

–All right.

He shuts the door again. Leave it, leave the light on in the pink room. No, no, must put it off. Must take a Calmpose and sleep. So that in the morning everyone finds him natural, normal.

Guard! What a valiant vigil you're keeping! Had a James Hadley Chase right here in the room. And you didn't see a thing.

He remembers Jamuna.

–You keep cash in the lopt!

Alas, Jamuna! Your first chance of a child, and you ended up dead. The cash stays here for two, three days at most. Then it moves into an anonymous account, numerous schemes, lays cash eggs and hatches cash babies. In the case of cash, the rules of family planning do not, cannot, apply.

Or else how will the price of Kolkata real estate keep rising? This is all black money, you touch it and there's bound to be a revolt.

I touched a corpse—should I take a bath?

Since Kumkum isn't here doing her daily pujas, there's no holy Ganga water that he can sprinkle over himself.

He goes to the bathroom, throws off all his clothes, wraps a silk lungi around himself. Rinses his hands and feet and face over and over again. Now to take a Calmpose and worship sleep.

Soft and white sheets and a bed of thorns.

When he shuts his eyes, Jamuna.

Sprawled on the carpet, Jamuna.

In the bathtub, Jamuna.

Everywhere Jamuna, Jamuna, Jamuna.

SEVEN

In the bathtub, Jamuna.

The sun has barely risen. Desai bites his lip, staring.

His flight from Bombay took off late, landed in the middle of the night. He spent the night at the airport. As soon as it was dawn, he took a taxi home. He was very worried. He had left Ila alone.

He hadn't rung the front doorbell. He'd entered through the back door. He always did that. Ila sleeps late due to her sleep medicine. This sleep of hers is very precious to him.

Ila lost her mental balance many years ago. Now, the more she sleeps, the better it is.

Ila, Ila would keep saying, Don't let that bitch enter my house. I'll kill her.

Saying 'I'll kill her' is one thing—but had she really gone and done it? What if this gets out? You'll be locked up with the criminal lunatics. And that is hell, hell, Ila!

I am always protecting you. Fly to Bombay in the morning to confer with our son, fly back that same night.

–I'll kill her.

–Why is she wearing Suchetana's clothes?

–She puts poison in my water.

–I'll finish her off too.

Jamuna, Jamuna! How many times had I told you, don't call memsahib 'the mad woman'. How, and to whom, can Desai explain all this?

He hadn't wanted to employ Jamuna. But Ila's insane, Ila threatens to kill everyone—so no one wants to work here.

Jamuna had agreed.

One hundred rupees salary, a warm wrap for winter, new clothes for Durga Puja. But she never missed a day of work.

No cook, no houseboy, food ordered in from restaurants, Ila completely crazy. It's only because of Jamuna that the house was clean, the dishes scrubbed, the clothes washed, the bottles filled with water from the filter.

And what has Ila done to that Jamuna? How did she do it?

Desai shuts the bathroom door. He also locks the door of the attached bedroom. As he does so, his eyes fall on Suchetana's smiling face.

Dressed as a bride, with a smile on her lips, Suchetana is staring at the camera. Everyone else will grow old, but she never will. She will always be twenty-two, always smiling, always sparkling in her bridal clothes and jewels.

Desai shuts the door. Locks it. Who could have imagined that within a year of their wedding both bride and groom would be killed in a plane crash?

When God chooses to bestow his blessings, he does so in abundance.

Desai was blessed, abundantly blessed. His only daughter, and her husband. The young man in turn had been the only child of his parents.

His wife lost her mental balance and went mad.

His only son, a doctor, lives in Bombay. He's too busy to visit. It's Desai who has to fly to him every time he wants to talk about Ila.

Slowly, slowly, Ila is taking a turn for the worse. It's impossible to make his son understand. Even though it is only after consulting his son that he was able to contact Dr Deshpande in Bombay, and get him to treat Ila a few times in Bombay itself. Ila has been in his nursing home too, a few times.

Of late, Ila has been saying 'I'll kill her' a bit too often, staring ferociously at everyone. For some reason she's obsessed with the idea that Jamuna has taken to wearing her daughter Suchetana's clothes.

Suchetana has been dead seven years. None of her clothes are in this house, she had never set eyes on Jamuna.

Who's to explain?

She tells him as well, I'll kill you.

He thinks, Why not, Ila. If you kill me, then I won't have to worry about you.

This time he had gone to Bombay to tell his son, Your mother has to be permanently moved into some kind of facility. It will have to be in Bombay.

–Why? Is there no improvement?

–No. No improvement.

–What are the symptoms?

–How do I explain?

–Does she keep talking to herself? Like she used to?

–Talking to herself, that was different. Nowadays . . . well, take a recent example. I brought her here, she went into a nursing home, she got a bit better, so I took her back . . .

–And then?

–I thought she'd got better, then I realized that she was saying, 'I'll kill you', 'I'll murder you' all the time. Yet she's so cunning, she looks elsewhere and speaks in a low voice while saying it . . .

–Is her anger directed at any particular person?

–What do you mean 'any particular person'?

–Servants or maids?

–She hurled a boiling kettle at the cook. How much it cost to settle that matter! Since then no one is willing to work, not even a sweeper. No one lasts.

–Baba! How do you manage?

–One maid comes part-time, I watch your mother day and night, order in food from a restaurant.

–It's very hard.

–Yes, it is. I'm also sixty-five now. At this age, to fly out in the morning, fly back in the evening, constantly worry about how she is . . .

–Yes. What should we do?

–We have to admit her permanently somewhere. Fix it up, call me and let me know. As soon as you tell me, I'll bring her here.

–When she left here, things were not so bad.

–Mentally-ill people also develop a keen cunning. She'll never let on what she's thinking. You're saying 'not so bad'! As soon as we landed in Dum Dum, she gave me such a kick that I fell flat. I didn't tell you, how much can I tell you anyway?

–Really, that Ma could become so . . .

–Talk to Deshpande.

–Will he keep her permanently?

–Why not? A single room, so she can be looked after. I'll give a donation, a big donation, what else should I save my money for?

–He'll charge a lot, Baba.

–I'm willing to pay. If I sell the Kolkata flat, I'll get at least fifteen lakhs for it. I'll take an advance, give the donation.

–No, no, you don't have to do that. Deshpande knows you won't default on the donation.

–Speak to him. It's urgent. Otherwise . . . Ila's aggression towards the maid could at any moment . . . neither of us wants a scandal. But that's exactly what can happen.

–No, no, I'll speak to him.

Yes, the boy's got frightened. If his mother does something like that, the dirt is bound to rub off on him too.

–Doesn't she mention Suchetana at all now?

–No. But recently she's started thinking that the maid is stealing Suchetana's clothes, wearing them.

–Incredible, that she hadn't gone mad then!

Desai thought of all this as he flew back home. Her only daughter went, her son-in-law went, at that time the fits of weeping, the silent withdrawal, were only natural.

Then, slowly, Ila seemed to come back to normal life. Started going again to her bonsai club, the handicapped children's welfare society, the 'Plant a Tree, Save Our City' club.

These last few years, she's given all that up. Begun to slowly lose her mind.

She won't mention her daughter, won't look at her photograph; she'll visit her son in Bombay but won't talk to him. The son is such an ass that he tells his father, Ma is different. She can never turn violent.

Come and see for yourself whether she's violent or not. Whether or not your sixty-year-old mother has murdered a twenty-something young woman and left her in the bathtub!

Desai mechanically goes into his bathroom, takes a bath. Comes out, makes coffee, drinks it.

Then he goes and stands beside Ila.

She's asleep, sound asleep. If anyone saw her now, could they imagine her capable of such a horrible act? One would think that after being tossed and turned by life's troubles, she had finally stepped onto shore and fallen asleep.

Desai sits, his head clutched in his hands. This room feels as empty as a crematorium.

His whole life is a crematorium.

Desai had amassed a lot of money speculating on the stock market. Even so, had it been wise to buy this flat? Grewal had sold it to him. Grewal's driver had run off with all his black money, or something like that. Grewal spent a lot of time and a lot of money to keep the police quiet. Then he sold him this flat and went off to Delhi.

They did up the flat just the way they'd always wanted. Ila used to get her share of the profits from her father's famous shirting–suiting business. There was no difficulty in doing it up.

One of the rooms even had a brass swing. The kind you see in Gujarat. It had been such a dream, that they'd swing on it, sitting side by side.

He was a sahib, Ila a memsahib, his son a double sahib, though Suchetana had been more Indian. Still, he was a man from Kathiawar, so let the swing remain as a memento. Desai's parents hadn't spoken to each other for years. Yet they spent hours in melancholy silence, sitting side by side on the swing.

The bed, table and chair in this room are handcrafted lacquer-ware. The bedcover is embroidered with mirrors.

The room has a distinct feel of Gujarat. As long as Ila had been all right, how many hours they'd spent side by side, gently swinging and talking.

After they bought this house, how many tragedies occurred?

Their son's motor accident—

The death of Suchetana and their son-in-law—

His own leg fracture—

Ila! Ila! Ila!

No, no, none of that happened because of the house. Whatever happened was because of something else. The brakes in his son's car failed. The airplane carrying Suchetana wasn't inspected properly before take-off. He broke his leg in a bad fall. As for Ila, perhaps her effort to stay so strong after Suchetana's death caused her to shatter inside.

Should he call the police?

No, no, no.

Involving the police means paying them off. Whatever family the girl has, they'll have to be paid too. All the newspapers will print juicy reports, and they'll take away Ila, send her to some horrible, hellish place.

No matter how shiny Barnamala appears to be, just a few steps away from its gates are all those areas of Khidirpur, how can one forget that?

The slums here are dens of anti-socials. Fights and murders are everyday fare. The stolen-goods trade is thriving. Vinod Mehta was murdered here. Fancy Market keeps multiplying. This is a whole other Kolkata.

Jamuna came from one of these slums. If those people get to know, will they let him go?

Kolkata has a different kind of temper altogether.

In the slums, they beat up one another.

But should one of the car-and-flat-owning, English-speaking lot dare lay a finger on one of them?

They'll leap on him as one.

There is no way you can explain to them that the murderer was a madwoman. They'd all say, Who keeps a lunatic like that at home?

To whom could he explain what a wonderful wife Ila had been, what a loving mother. How well spoken she was, how well behaved.

He too no longer had any connection with his neighbours in this building.

All gone because of Ila.

Should he turn to Arjun-babu? His wife is the only one from whom Ila occasionally borrows a book. Doesn't read it, she can't. The wife isn't home either.

But what can Arjun-babu do?

Nowadays no one wants to get into somebody else's problems. And it's impossible, anyway. He doesn't know a single person who can help him with the problem of murder.

No need, no need. Whatever Ila has done was not done knowingly. One can't push her into the lion's jaws for this. She must be protected.

Suddenly Desai realizes that Ila is awake.

–Hi, Ila!

–Hi, Dhiru.

–Won't you get up?

–Aren't you and I leaving for Kashmir today? Where are our clothes? Where are the suitcases?

–It'll all get done.

–Our clothes . . . she must've stolen them.

–Who?

–That bitch! Jamuna!

–Ila, did you do something to her?

–No I haven't, but I will kill her for sure.

–Did you give her something to eat?

Ila smiles a very cunning smile.

–Why should I? The two of us ate dinner together, drank together, how she can drink!

–Where did you get the drink?

–She brings some every day, we drink together.

–Did you mix something in it?

–Why should I say? Why should I tell you? She's stolen all Suchetana's saris, all my jewellery. I'll crush her to death with my own hands.

Ila sits up. Desai, seated at a distance, watches her closely. Salt and pepper hair. Since she's lost her mind, she wears shorts and T-shirts. Arms quite long, shoulders broad, big boned.

Those two arms could easily have lifted Jamuna and deposited her in the bathtub. The insane are possessed of great strength, too.

But which room did she carry her from?

–Which room did you eat in?

–Dining room. Not in the bathroom, surely!

–What did you eat?

–Don't remember.

–Did you take your medicine?

–Those medicines are no good. The girl gets me pure stuff straight from the docks.

–What stuff? Won't you tell me?

–No. Then you'll beat me.

–Have I ever laid a finger on you?

–Of course! You beat me every day!

–Have I beaten you today?

–You beat me last night.

–Last night I was in Dum Dum.

–Lies!

–When did Jamuna come, Ila?

–Won't tell, won't tell!

–Why not?

–Make the coffee, make the toast.

–I'm doing it, Ila, doing it.

What could Ila have given her? Where did she get it? Ila! What if you hadn't given it to her? What if you had taken it yourself? Desai has heard that the night guard's son gets stuff from the docks, supplies the flats. Could she have got it from him?

No point thinking about it. Desai just can't figure out how Ila could have killed her. The sum of it is: Ila is insane, she hated Jamuna. Yesterday Ila was left alone for about twenty-four hours, although there was plenty of sleep medication mixed into her drinking water, into her thermos of orange juice. That has to be done. How else can he leave the house?

Ila had been alone.

Jamuna was in the bathtub.

Although it's impossible to follow what Ila is talking about now.

–Drink your coffee, Ila, take your toast.

–Give.

After finishing her toast and coffee Ila suddenly shrieks, Why is it so bitter? What have you fed me? Why are you poisoning me?!

–Ila!

–Conspiracy! Conspiracy! Help! Help!

Desai clamps her mouth shut. Gives her a tight slap. Forces her flat on the bed, holds her down. Such a strong sedative, it has to have an effect. Deshpande has been a big help. Such a powerful sedative, yet hardly any taste. Very effective.

Ila calms down. Once she's calm, Deshpande administers the injection. Tears fall from Ila's eyes. When he gives her the injection and sees tears in her eyes, his heart aches fit to burst. But Ila! This is for your own good! Go to sleep, stay unconscious, only then can I save you.

Ila is a madwoman, granted. So when she screams 'Help! Help!' people may well turn a deaf ear. But in such apartments, if someone truly in danger were to yell for help, would the neighbours ever come running to the rescue?

Lots to do today. Will Ila have to be kept sedated through the day? It won't be possible to move Jamuna till late at night. Where will he move her to? He has to think of how he will move her. First, move Jamuna. Then, a few days later, he'll take Ila to Bombay and submit her to permanent exile in Deshpande's mental home. Then he'll sell off the Kolkata flat and go stay somewhere in Bombay. Not with his son. Unless he lives in Bombay, how will he see Ila?

Now, where else did Jamuna work?

At Arjun-babu's place! And at No. 11. Yes, No. 11.

The caretaker at No. 11 is Mohsin. The main door and back door of that flat are flanked by tubs of evergreens. Mohsin and Jamuna, sitting in that corridor, laughing, smoking cigarettes, he's seen it all. Jamuna had no morals. As uncouth as she was uneducated. Actually, if she'd died somewhere else, Desai wouldn't have given it a second thought. It's because she's dead in his flat that he's having to think so much about her.

Anyway, he should go to the balcony. He spends about ten minutes there every day, jogging. He should follow his routine, or people will grow suspicious. Desai doesn't want that.

Balconies facing each other.

Desai is jogging for the same reason that Arjun is also jogging. One must remain normal in one's actions and behaviour. As soon as he sees Desai, Arjun realizes why the old man is jogging despite getting home only at the crack of dawn and entering through the back door.

Arjun is elated. He had smuggled his Jamuna into that man's house. But can you see any sign of that on his face? What a dangerous old man, this Desai!

–Hi!

–Hi!

–So when can we expect to hear the good news?

–A month or so to go.

–Good, very good.

–How is Mrs Desai?

–The same.

–I heard on the radio, last night there was a sudden thunderstorm in Bombay.

–You're telling me! That's why my flight was so late. I always worry about Ila, you see.

–Where did you go?

–Where else? Bombay.

–To your son?

–Son, Ila's doctor . . .

–Flying out in the morning, flying back at night . . .

–It's the jet age!

–Not going out today?

–No. Ila's health is . . .

–Really. The way you look after her, it's so rare these days.

–We've been married forty years. For nearly thirty-four years, it was Ila who took care of me. Can't I take care of her for a few years?

–I might have to go to Haldia for a few days.

–The missus is with her parents?

–Yes, it's best for her at this stage. To have children at this age . . .

–Don't worry, Arjun-babu. My sister had her first child at thirty-two. After thirteen years of marriage. And those were different times. Science hadn't progressed as much.

–I, worry about her? She's the one who's always worrying about me! How is the house running, what are you eating, how this, how that!

–Wives! It's their job to worry!

–You're so right. Hang on, I think Bahadur is trying to ask you something.

–What is it, Bahadur?

–Desai-sahib, Mohsin from No. 11 is asking if Jamuna's come to work? She didn't go to them last evening either.

Arjun quickly says, She hasn't come to my flat. Desai, has she come to yours?

Desai responds with astounding ease, She didn't come last evening, I can tell by the state of the house. She hasn't shown up yet, though she doesn't come to us till much later. And we all know there's no point in checking with my wife.

Arjun says, Bahadur, tell him she hasn't come to either of our houses, at least not yet.

Bahadur goes away.

Arjun's mind says, Desai, I salute you! Jamuna's in your bathtub, and yet you speak so calmly! If you really came back from Bombay, you must have come in through that door, you must have seen her.

Or didn't you? Did you enter through the front? Anyway, you have no idea that I'm the one who planted her there.

No, Arjun is totally safe. If Mohsin is asking . . .

And is Mohsin any less of a rascal? Jamuna has told Arjun everything.

Jamuna would say, What a crazy guy! Says to me, Come on, let's get married.

Arjun would be very close to Jamuna then, stroking her back. She'd say something like that and he'd be shocked.

–Jamuna, don't you already have a husband?!

–He also has a wife.

–But, Jamuna, he's a Mussalman!

–Die, you bastard! So what if he's Muslim? If I want to, I'll run away with him. Just that I'm waiting for my husband to come back, so I haven't said yes.

–Chhi, chhi! Shame, a Mussalman.

–You're a Hindu—what do you do for your gods?

–Still, a Mussalman!

Jamuna had been sitting with her back against the wall. Mohsin is madly in love with me, she'd said. Whenever guests come, he feeds me chicken, pulao, whatever there is. He's not a bad man like you. Never laid a hand on me. The other day, he gave me biryani!

–No wonder you're so healthy!

–Mohsin feeds and nurtures the horse—and you, a gentleman! a babu!—you mount it! Just wait! Your death will be at my hands for sure, you maggot!

–Language, Jamuna, language!

–What's wrong with my bloody language?!

–Don't be so crude.

–Huh! I'll be as crude and as rude as I want.

–Chhi chhi, Jamuna! I . . . you . . .

–What? You give me money?

–I do that too.

–And so you should. I'm no free fuck.

–I love you.

–Very good! Let Boudi come home with the baby. In front of her I'll say, Boudi, your husband is in love with me. I'm your co-wife.

–Don't do that, Jamuna!

–Please the wife, ruin the maid—you gentlemen deserve a good thrashing!

Now, suddenly Arjun thinks, What if Mohsin's responsible for Jamuna's condition? What if he's the one who poisoned her?

Never mind, forget it. What's done is done, what's the point in thinking about it, in prodding a snake?

I framed Desai. That's not right. But I have to save myself, after all!

Desai keeps jogging. And says, Have to take the missus to Bombay. The son's been saying, Let Ma stay with me.

–You have a dutiful son.

–Yes, he's a good boy.

–And why wouldn't he be? All of us regard you as the ideal husband. Feel so sad about your wife. Who could have thought she'd become like this? Such life! Such energy! Sure to step up for any good cause!

–That's always been her way. Never met anyone like her, never will.

–It's all fate.

–Not fate, Arjun-babu. Ila is unwell. This is her illness. In our country, its treatment hasn't advanced at all. Nor are there any decent arrangements for such patients. And yet this illness is multiplying. See what it's like in America. Even the small towns have facilities for people like her. Many countries have them.

–India simply shuts its eyes, sleeps.

–True.

–Kumkum really praises you!

–She is like my daughter. If Suchetana had lived, they would have been around the same age. All right, I'll be off now. See you soon.

Desai's going to take his wife to Bombay? To stay with his son? But the son has never come to see his mother. You're the one who goes to him. Maybe this time he'll admit her permanently somewhere. Do that. It's impossible to live with a mad woman.

What will you do now?

Isn't Jamuna in your bathtub?

Arjun-babu is thinking. Weighed on the scales, who is more fortunate, he or Desai? It seems that the scales are tipped in his favour.

Jamuna is in Desai's flat.

Jamuna is not in Arjun's flat.

Ila Desai is completely mad.

Kumkum is not mad.

Ila Desai wears shorts and T-shirts.

Kumkum wears saris.

Desai's life is dark.

In Arjun's life, Jupiter is shining bright. The contractors' trade is thriving, is thriving, will thrive!

Now he must proceed with caution. No more taking medication that makes him lose control. And never again employing a youthful maid.

He must inform Keshtokali.

He'll say nothing on the telephone. He'll go himself, tell him, No arrangements needed after all, my friend. All that was Jamuna's miscalculation. The problem has solved itself.

Anyway. It's a huge relief that Jamuna's no longer in his house.

He'll spend all his time with Kumkum. It's important to keep her happy. Kumkum is his Lakshmi, bountiful goddess of his home and his business. In his heart, he still feels deeply for her.

After ages, he'll go to Mandolina Bar this evening. His friends will be there. He hasn't had a drink with them in a long time.

It's been so long since he got back home completely drunk. He'll drink tonight and come home really late.

Ah night! Dark night! Desai, you'll seek out the night too, you'll have to. What state will Jamuna be in by then?

You die, Desai, I'll stay alive. My staying alive is vital.

Arjun goes back in and takes a bath with great pleasure. Nothing feels as good as a bath.

When he emerges from the bathroom, Mohini looks at him and says, in an expressionless voice, What should I cook? Better tell me at one go. It takes time to cook, and you'll want to eat before you leave, yes?

–No, no, I have to go out. No need for any food. I'll have dinner out, too.

–So much stuff in the fridge. Ilish, mutton, vegetables, rice!

–Clear it out, take it all.

–Jamuna hasn't come, the rooms aren't done. What's happened to the girl?

–Let the rooms be. Take out the food, quickly. I'm in a hurry.

–How will I carry it all?

–Figure it out.

Mohini heaves a sigh. Then happily begins to clear out the fridge. These babus and their strange ways. All this food fit for the gods, and he'll eat none of it? Don't eat. Mohini and her family will eat. Happily eat it all.

Why hasn't Jamuna come?

For some days now she's had a long face, no interest in her work. She was having such a good time with babu. Do you think Mohini can't tell? Using Boudi's soap, her shampoo, her towels.

Doing all this just because babu's got the hots for you. Mohini had warned her, Don't get ahead of yourself, Jamuna, you won't be able to handle it.

Jamuna had said, What can I do, aunt? That maggot is the one gobbling me up.

–I don't know, my child.

–Slime! Old lech!

What does it mean, he gobbled her up? Yesterday morning when Jamuna came, her face was hard and grim. She shut the door and argued loudly with babu. Altogether, it can only mean one thing. Mohini's no fool. Anyway, let it be. Why worry about Jamuna? She's busy taking all the rice, dal, oil, groceries, etc.

Bahadur doesn't take anything. Just watches it all. Babu is very open handed. Boudi too. Money, clothes, what don't they give? They give everything.

Packing it all up, Mohini says, I'm off, babu. We'll need to go to the market tomorrow morning.

–Yes, see you.

Arjun prances quickly around the empty flat. Bahadur is a good lad. He's tidied and made the bed. Put his cast-off clothes into the laundry basket. If not tomorrow, then the day after, another maid . . .

Driving away in his car, Arjun never thinks for a moment about the key Jamuna had to the flat, and where it may be now.

*

Desai enters the flat. Then emerges, looking for the sweeper. Sees him coming out of the house opposite.

–Salaam, sa'ab.

–Yes, listen jamadar, can you tell the restaurant not to deliver food to our house today?

–Why, won't y'all eat?

–Ma-ji's not feeling well, and neither am I.

–You have such a hard time because of Ma-ji, Sa'ab.

Desai smiles sadly. It's all fate, jamadar. What can I do?

–A puja or something . . .

–Let's see.

As soon as the sweeper leaves, Desai goes into the guest-room. Shuts the door, locks it, then enters the bathroom.

91

Just as he'd thought. The light stench of rotting flesh, the belly now swollen, the body oozing fluids. What an unbelievable situation.

Should he sprinkle some phenyl?

No, no, he'll spread a polythene sheet in the middle of the guestroom. The bed, table, cupboard everything is covered in thick polythene anyway. In case Suchetana ever comes back . . .

He'll lay Jamuna down on a polythene sheet on the guestroom floor. Put a towel under her head. Stuff cottonwool in her mouth, ears, nostrils. Run the air cooler and the fan.

He'll do it all. He can't put Ila in danger, impossible. He can do anything to protect Ila.

Desai had never in his life imagined that he was capable of such things. His life so far had never needed him to be. But when the need arises, you just do it.

He lays down the polythene sheet. Then, holding his breath, he lifts that heavy, terribly heavy body and places it on the sheet. Tucks a thick Turkish towel under the head. Strange smell, so strange! Suchetana's smiling face watches her father.

For your mother's sake, my dear! I have no hand in this!

After death, the corpse is first soft, then rigid, then soft again. Jamuna had just about reached the third stage.

Dried moisture at the corner of her eyes. It would be best if he could shift her now, but that's not possible. Turn them on, the air cooler, the fan. Should he wipe her down with spirit? The belly's a bit bloated. It will bloat more.

After sorting out Jamuna, Desai washes down the bath tub with phenyl.

He had lots to do. Sprinkle Odonil in the bathroom and room. So much to do, Ila! You have to be injected with your sedative again. Not eating for a day or two will do you no harm.

Why, why did you kill her, Ila? What did you use? Did you kill her, or did someone else . . .

Today, you sleep all day. Tonight I'll smuggle her out, clean the guestroom, tomorrow morning I'll bathe you, feed you. After I've kept you unconscious like this, I can handle you better.

Tomorrow I'll call the local doctor. Keep you in his nursing home for the time being. Then make a trunk call to Bombay and take you there.

A sour stink assails him as he enters the dining room. Tiffin carrier open, scattered leftovers, slowly rotting.

He cleans it a–l–l, every bit of it. Makes the flat spick and span. For some years now, he has grown accustomed to doing all this work himself.

He places the garbage outside in the corridor, in the covered waste bin. The sweeper will take it away. Because of Ila, no sweeper enters this house. Now he thinks, just as well.

It helps him that the liftman, sweepers, maids and servants are all sympathetic to him. In the history of Barnamala, there is no other instance of so great a self-sacrifice by a husband for a mad wife.

The maids say, Such lifetimes of penance the memsahib must have done to get a husband like this! But she couldn't hold on to it, couldn't enjoy her good fortune.

Then he has another bath. Opens the fridge, takes out a can of tomato soup, some bread, makes some coffee. Sits at the table and eats.

Mohsin, Mohsin, someone's framed me, now I'll frame you. You'll get entangled with the police, be in deep trouble. Forgive me, Mohsin, I have to do this to save Ila.

Those who have designed these flats deserve to be congratulated. The guestroom bathroom in every flat is near the lift—for the sweeper, maids, servants to come and go. The lights there are dim. If he can somehow drag it down that corridor to No. 11, then he's safe.

Then let Mohsin do what he will.

EIGHT

Mohsin couldn't figure out what was going on.

It's all very suspicious. Jamuna came yesterday late in the afternoon, swaying on her feet, her face and eyes so strange. Leaning against the doorframe, she said, Can't come to work today, re! Body's feeling ill, head's reeling. What a medicine that Lame Doctor's given me!

–Why did you need his medicine?

–For the same reason women always do.

–Oh!

–I'll go and rest in babu's flat, let's see if I feel better. I feel like everything's burning.

–I loved you so much, re, Jamuna, you never knew how much. That babu . . .

–It's all burning, like acid! Who else can I tell but you?

–You didn't have faith in me!

–It's all going, re! See, I didn't listen to you. Then the babu also . . . I just kept waiting for that useless sod . . . my whole life's been washed away.

–Don't talk like that.

–I'll wait one more month. If he's still not back, I'll go away with you.

–Really?

–Really, really, really.

Something made Jamuna, with deep affection, caress Mohsin's pock-marked face over and over again.

–Who else loves me but you?

–That Arjun-babu . . .

–That blood-sucking leech! I'm off.

–How will you get in?

–I have a key, don't I?

Jamuna fished out a key from her blouse, tied up in a hanky, and showed it to him. Jamuna! Jamuna! Mohsin knows everything—where you enter from, what you're up to. And still he feels true love for you. True love is a very pure thing. Mohsin and Jamuna have eaten together, smoked together, but Mohsin has never dishonoured her, hasn't so much as laid a finger on her till now.

Jamuna for some reason kept talking, in fits and starts, You're not like the rest . . . the others only want one thing . . . Got myself in trouble, otherwise . . . I'll get so much money, Mohsin. You and I, we'll go off somewhere and open a shop. He won't come back, so my heart keeps telling me . . .

Jamuna left. Showed me her key, said, I'll go and lie down there.

But she hasn't come out again.

Why did babu say that she hasn't come to work? Of course she hasn't come. If she hasn't come to the mad lady's house, Arjun-babu's house, Mohsin's house—then she hasn't come to work, that's for sure.

But there's no doubt that she went to Arjun-babu's place yesterday.

Mohsin is a witness to that.

So did she leave at night?

Deep within Mohsin, the real Mohsin keeps raising his head, considers everything with fierce suspicion. This is not the Mohsin who is the caretaker of a tobacco company's guesthouse. This Mohsin is the one-time foot soldier of the docklands.

Every one of Barnamala's workers has come through the same private-employment agency. Agency: meaning, one Special Person. He was the anonymous king of this locality. You can't do a thing without him. Anyone who's tried has paid for it with their lives.

The management office of this and many other multi-storey buildings have an ongoing arrangement with this Special Person. These days, Special Person has moved beyond taking care of the nuts and bolts. Still, for those who had spent years working for him, it was his duty to find them jobs.

Many people had never set eyes on him. For years now, he's slept all day long.

Six in the evening was the crack of dawn for him.

He'll wake up, wash his face, drink creamy tea. Then brush his teeth, do the daily job, bathe. Breakfast at seven.

Poppy seeds, raisins, almonds, walnuts.

Then sit in session.

A map of Khidirpur pasted on the wall, him on a carpet on the floor. Guards at the door.

Talk of work, business, accounts. Punishment for some, rewards for others, as required.

He has been quiet for a while now. But the world won't let him stay on the right path.

Some smuggled goods dispatched, some sold off. Cocaine to gold. Medical chemicals to electronic gadgets. Gun parts to baby food.

Many people call him a criminal, anti-social.

Many call him a saviour.

He merely points to the heavens. Whatever is done is by His will alone. Special Person is no more than a mere speck in it all.

This is not the time for toil.

This is the time to sit still.

Even so, he has many people's jobs to think about. Can they just be cut adrift? The slums are all his. For example, Barnamala and the other multi-storey blocks are all on his land. One way or another, he's managed to place his people in all of them. Mohsin is disturbed, very disturbed.

What to tell Special Person? He knows everything. Quite some time ago, he'd told Mohsin with such affection, You can marry that girl if you want. But you have a wife. Get her consent, make proper arrangements for her, then go ahead. Or else . . .

Mohsin abruptly sets off in search of the management-office guard.

He's not there.

He'll have to go to Jamuna's home, he must. But how? For some days now, the boss' close friend has been staying incognito at the tobacco company guesthouse.

Once a year this fool goes into hiding. He's a writer. As soon as it's time for the Puja magazine submissions, apparently he needs to be absolutely alone. The boss has quite a fetish for things like this. He has a house in some foreign land. Travels abroad constantly. But he has a terrible weakness for singers, musicians, writers, artists.

Apparently, the boss used to write poetry once.

And once a year, the boss unfailingly burdens Mohsin with this chap. And so many instructions.

No visitors. He won't go anywhere.

Scotch, chicken, whatever and whenever he wants it.

He is very, very famous.

And strange too. Every now and then he makes Mohsin jump out of his skin.

–What is *obligation*?

–In autumn, do flowers bloom in Baruipur?

–What goes on in the docks at night?

–Do you love that girl? What's the matter? She has a husband, you have a wife, but Mohsin, love is god. You must surrender to it.

–My thirst for love hasn't been quenched, Mohsin! I still haven't found love . . .

Just listen to the man! Wife, son, daughter-in-law, son-in-law, ten grandchildren! How much more love does the old man want!

Who knows when he'll call for Mohsin, ask him, When will the mango blossoms begin to bud? That's why Mohsin's stuck here. And then there's the boss himself, bottle in hand, showing up without any warning.

Foreign stuff for the writer. He's such a close friend, after all!

And how the two of them talk!

–When are you going to write about me?

–I will, I will.

–When?

–You're in the thick of life right now. Write your own life first, then I'll take over . . .

–Oh, this life is endless, endless . . .

–Drink it to the lees . . .

–Yes. Mohsin! More ice!

The man wants Chinese today, Mughlai tomorrow, Continental the day after. Mohsin would share all of it with Jamuna. All of it. Jamuna would eat with him. Call her husband 'prick' in one tone of voice. And Arjun-babu a 'prick' in another.

She told this guest one day, Babu, you're a real prick, you are! Jabbering away to me, and winking at the same time too?

But he didn't get angry.

–Forgive me, forgive me, Jamuna . . . whenever I see you, I . . .

–Get turned on, do you? You old cock!

–No, no, I mean to say, I start thinking of my daughter . . .

–Who is she to me?

–She . . . is . . . er . . .

–Out of my way, please. Let me clean the room.

–'Cock', 'prick', I'm telling you, Mohsin. Unless this language of the common man comes into literature, literature will never be free! Due to excessive chastity, Bengali literature is not only in confinement, it's also riddled with disease!

Jamuna said, Really, babu! No worries about food or clothing. Take two puffs of a cigarette and chuck it away. Drink foreign booze. And so clever with words he is too!

–Jamuna, Jamuna, so incomparable you are!

–Really, babu, the games you people play!

That man too had seen Jamuna yesterday. Should Mohsin ask him? He wants to go out, but he can't just yet, not until it's late into the night. The boss might come, the boss' wife might come . . .

The wife was a fatty. Went to a clinic, became slim and trim. Cut her hair, started wearing pants, what style!

In front of her husband, she calls the fellow 'Alok-babu'.

Behind her husband's back, what a coy act! Alok, Alok, tell me, how often did you think of me today?

–All the time!

–Eesh! Only roses in this room! How will you ever be able to write, Alok? How?

–You're no less a flower yourself!

–Oh, Alok, Alok!

The husband could show up. The wife could show up. And if Mohsin's missing, there goes his job.

Mohsin feels a bit off. Actually, he needs the guard from the office downstairs. He's the Special Person's man. Has infinite powers. Opening any kind of lock is child's play to him.

In the matter of Jamuna and Mohsin, he's on Mohsin's side.

–Hey, you, girl. It's the luck of seven generations that an honest man like Mohsin loves you.

–Get lost. I have a husband, don't I?

–No.

–No meaning?

–How many years you been married?

–Four.

–Done the proper way, puja and all?

–Kalighat wedding.

–Arrey, four years married, still not a mother. False marriage.

–Don't talk rubbish.

–The guy's no good either.

–How would you know!

–Arrey, only a fool loses his job by doing union. Want to do union, then be a leader, earn double, not—

This hits Jamuna hard. Exhaling sharply, she says, You're so right. Dock lands so close by, so many options. Couldn't he choose a line? But no, the same old thing. Honest living, honest living!

–Same old thing.

Mohsin has no option but to say, Babu, I'll be back in a bit—and go down again. The guard says, What news?

–Captain-da!

–What's happened?

–Come this side.

–Why? Jamuna run off?

–You . . . did you see Jamuna come, yesterday evening?

–I did.

–Did you see her leave?

–No I didn't. Didn't really notice.

–Listen.

–Not now, my boy. Got work.

–When will you get off duty?

–Nine o' clock.

–Just come up for a bit, once? Have a drink of some foreign stuff?

–Of course. I'll come.

Mohsin goes back upstairs. Let Captain Singh come. He'll coax and cajole him into staying here for an hour or so. Then Mohsin can go to Jamuna's home.

Arjun-babu's flat is shut up, silent as the grave.

Mad Memsahib's husband is sitting on his balcony, smoking a cheroot. Poor fellow. Unlucky old man. The old woman losing her mind at this age! He's a really good man, that's for sure. How devotedly he looks after his wife.

So many doctors come, try out so many remedies.

Mohsin thinks, Why does Khudatala dole out so much suffering even to such good men?

Mohsin doesn't think about his own wife.

She married him when she was fourteen. Then all of sudden began to look thirty-four. Yet how old would she be now? Just about twenty-five?

Half dead from chronic acidity and indigestion, their boy's being raised by Mohsin's sister and brother-in-law.

Jamuna, Jamuna, you girl sharp as a knife. Tongue sharp as a knife too.

The writer asks, What's happened?

–Why, babu?

–You seem a bit sad.

–It's personal, babu.

–Jamuna hasn't come today?

–No, she hasn't.

–Look. Maybe her husband is back.

Mohsin, laying out food on the table, says, What husband, babu?

–Why? She has a husband, doesn't she?

–Just being married doesn't make you a husband, babu.

–How true! Well said.

–Doesn't give her love, leaves her and goes off . . . Jamuna is a very unhappy woman, babu.

–The sweeper said something about brothers . . .

–They are not her blood brothers, babu. But what else can Jamuna do? A young woman, living in a place like this, how can she survive without potecshun?

–So what do these brothers-by-choice do?

–Nothing immoral.

–In this area . . .

–What about this area? Do crimes happen only in the slums? Nothing bad happens in the fancy homes?

–No, no, it's not that . . .

–There's good everywhere. Bad everywhere. Jamuna is a very good girl, babu.

–You really do love her, truly love her. One doesn't see that often.

–She's a silly girl. Can't tell what's good for her and what's not. And no control over her tongue. Says whatever comes into her mind.

–Maybe her husband isn't back. Maybe she's sick or something.

–Sick!

Mohsin thinks, That's it! Yesterday she was unwell. Then is she still lying sick in A-babu's flat?

No, no, then Bahadur would have told me.

Then has the news reached already? To that one room, far off, at the other end of the earth?

What had she said? Lame Doctor's medicine . . .

–Babu, can I go for a bit?

–Where? To look for her?

–Yes, babu. I'll be back real quick. If Sir or Madam come . . .

–I'll tell them your wife is very ill. That you've gone to see her.

–Allah will bless you, sir.

–How old are you, Mohsin?

–I was born in the year of Hindustan–Pakistan. Ma used to say.

–Thirty-eight years! It can happen, love can happen at this age too. Love has no age limit, after all.

–Can't stop thinking about her, babu.

–Go, go, you carry on.

–Let me clear the table first.

–Leave it.

–No, babu, if Sir sees . . .

While he is cleaning up, Captain Singh bustles in.

His name is not Captain, his surname is not Singh. But when Special Person was building his private army, Ram Sahu, the ex-colliery thug, became Captain Singh.

Special Person got him a ration card in the name of Captain Singh. In this building, the guard, liftman, sweeper all wear brand-new khaki-green uniforms. Captain even wears expensive shoes.

–What's up, my boy?

–I'll tell you.

But he doesn't tell him. Thinks, if there's anything to tell Captain, I can tell him later. Right now, I should go look for her.

–Come, dada. Drink up.

Mohsin hands him a bottle of the boss' foreign booze. Says, I have to go out for a bit, dada. I'll come back and tell you everything. Go on, enjoy yourself.

–Looking for Jamuna?

–Yes, dada.

–Go. Get the girl back. I'll get you two married. Go on. As for me, I've got my sweetheart right here.

Mohsin and Captain go downstairs together. Captain says, The babu in No. 11's a good guy. Wife's old and mad. But how he looks after her.

–A very good man.

–That's the way it is. For every nine devils, there'll be one saint. That's the way of the world.

–Yes, dada.

–What news of Johnny and Tala?

–Who knows?

–Such a sweet pair.

–All sorts in this world.

Once he's past the building gates, Mohsin almost breaks into a run. He doesn't go anywhere near his own home. The slum is now an enormous labyrinth. If you don't know it, you can't get through it.

Every corner. Every lamp post. The occasional sickly tree, that sewer, that pond, silent witnesses to so many incidents. So many corpses, so many fights, so many times the police cars, sirens shrieking, rushing in, then stopping. Lame Doctor's shop is shut.

–Hey, Laltu, where's the doctor, the cripple?

–Who knows?

–Seen Johnny and Tala?

–Gone to the movies.

–When?

–Night show.

A lock on Jamuna's door. A light in the next room. Ghulam's mother lives there.

–Oh, chachi!

–Who's that? Mohsin?

–Yes, it's me.

–At this time?

–Any news of Jamuna?

–No, my son. Why, didn't she go to work?

–No. Could she be sick . . .

–Sick how? I think she got what was coming to her. That floozy, throwing up every morning. I knew right away.

–Haven't seen her today?

–No, no. I've been home all day.

–She didn't go with Johnny and Tala?

–No, no. Ghulam, Johnny, Tala, they've all gone to a night show.

–Jamuna's . . . husband hasn't come, has he?

–No, no. Do you think he'll come? Jamuna says she's waiting for him. He would've come by now if he'd wanted to.

–Strange! Didn't show up at work either . . .

The old lady sighs. Maybe she's run off with someone. Young woman like her, how long will she sit around?

–No, no, she's not like that.

–Then maybe she's gone somewhere to get rid of the thorn.

Mohsin walks back lost in thought. Didn't go home, her husband hasn't come, what the old lady said about . . .

He'll have to speak to Captain.

Should he tell him? What if . . .

When he gets back to the flat, he finds the writer pacing about. He stops at the sight of Mohsin's face.

–Didn't find her?

–No, babu.

–Not at home?

–No.

–No one knows anything?

–No.

–Husband not back?

–No, babu.

–So what will you do?

–What can I do?

–Want to tell the police?

–No, no, babu, what can the police do?

–She has no mother or father?

–No, no, she has no one. You go to sleep, babu. Whatever has to happen will happen.

Out of habit, Mohsin shuts up the house, locks the doors and windows. Sees to the dirty dishes in the kitchen.

Then turns off the lights and lies down in the dining room.

His mind keeps going to the back corridor. The corridor down which Jamuna walked away, yesterday.

Throwing up! Lame Doctor's potion! Yes, Jamuna had been wearing babu's wife's nylon saris a lot of late.

Once she'd even brought Mohsin a whole bottle.

Says she's waiting for her husband, but is so friendly with Mohsin, and then there's that babu!

Very shifty babu. With a very dicey business. Or else why does he pay for special security?

Oh, how annoyed Captain is with some of these houses! Hiring a guard when we are there! Don't have any faith in us!

All that guard does is sit at his post and sleep.

What a good time that babu is having! His wife is with child, his business is expanding, and at the sight of his maid he . . .

Jamuna used to work in his house.

No. 7, Arjun-babu, this No. 11, and No. 19.

The No. 19 lot have gone to America. That leaves three flats.

Thinking and wondering, thinking and wondering, Mohsin falls asleep. But it's an uneasy slumber.

She entered babu's house, did she vanish or what?

Is this some djinn-fairy tale?

This building has a nasty history too. Maids have died mysterious deaths in the past as well.

This babu is talking of the police!

Arrey, how is the relationship between the rich folk and the police? Like man and wife. Can't brew beer without yeast. They can't survive without the police.

All those maids who died before, was anyone's death properly investigated?

The babu in No. 21 just . . .

How come Mohsin wasn't so concerned at the time when those cases occurred? Of course they talked about it among themselves: what was to happen has happened, what else?

Captain said, Arrey, in thief–dacoit cases, the police always take money from the bosses and goons and hush it up. Give them some money, they'll cover up even their own mother's murder! What do they care about the death of some maid!

Why does he think of death when he thinks of Jamuna?

Mohsin shivers in his sleep.

And on his eyelids comes and perches Jamuna. What a lush and lovely woman, my god, so lush and lovely!

Roundish face, large eyes, a small forehead, hair swept up, cascading down her back.

These breasts. These buttocks. This waist you can span with one hand. When she walks, like a full pitcher, brimming over.

Jamuna says, Hey, you good-for-nothing, you! Oh, Mohsin! Killing yourself looking for me? Search and search until he dies / whoever finds me, I'm his prize!

–Where are you?

–Damn! Play acting! No time for that, I'm off!

So she says, but Jamuna doesn't go anywhere.

Mohsin stretches out his hand, gropes in the air, breaks out in a sweat and sits up.

What was that? A dream? Mohsin touches the talisman at his throat.

Let me get up, wash my face and eyes, drink some water. But my limbs feel heavy, numb. I'll get up, open the door— why open the door?

Why can't I move my hands, my feet? That dream of Jamuna—she seemed more real than in real life.

Clutching the talisman, he gets up. Softly opens the kitchen door. Splashes water on his face, in his eyes.

It's very late. 1.30. Mohsin drinks some water.

Then he opens the door.

NINE

As Mohsin opens the door, Desai soundlessly shuts his own. He's sweating rivulets, sweating nonstop.

He hadn't left Jamuna wrapped in a polythene sheet, that would have given him away.

Desai felt he'd spent ten million years pulling and pulling, tugging and tugging the polythene-wrapped body down the ten-foot-long corridor, aged ten million years too.

He'd wrapped a hanky around each hand. His hands had been sinking into Jamuna's flesh. Even though the air cooler and fan had helped quite a bit.

Where did he get the strength? How did he manage to drag her so far?

Mohsin's corridor had a few rubber plants, a few evergreens. He laid her down there, unwrapped the polythene.

Tiptoed back to his own bathroom and hurled the polythene sheet into the bathtub in disgust.

Quietly mopped the corridor, all the way up to the bathroom door.

Then shut the door again. This time, he locked it.

Desai opened the guestroom windows. Put off the air cooler, left only the fan on. Wiped down the floor with phenyl. Let the stench, the stench of Jamuna, disperse, disappear. Sprinkled Odonil everywhere.

Soaking the polythene sheet in soap water in the tub, he thinks: Now I'll have to bathe in this bathroom itself. Wash the polythene really well. Wash my vest and pyjamas too, after my bath, and hang them here to dry.

Desai does it a—ll, but his ears are pricked for sound from that side. Is there any sound from Mohsin's place? No, all is quiet. Desai found Jamuna in his bathtub. Moved her to Mohsin's flat. If Mohsin finds her, he'll have to move her too. If he doesn't find her, he'll be in trouble.

Was there any other way for Desai to save Ila? Even if there is some doubt over what Ila could have poisoned her with, it's also true that Ila will be the first to say, I killed her. And with her insane cunning, she'll narrate the full story of how exactly she murdered her.

He knows that if there is a case, if a full investigation is done, it may be proved some day that Ila did or did not commit this murder.

But the publicity? As soon as the case is registered, all that publicity?

No, Desai can't take any more risks. He's protected Ila all these years, he'll protect her now as well. Ila will go to Deshpande's mental home. He will sell this flat, wrap up his business. Look for a place to stay in Bombay. He knows his son well, how often will he visit his mother?

He'll have to give it all up. The flat, furniture, swing, beautiful kitchen. For now, he'll phone the local doctor in the morning. Let her stay in Dr Gupta's nursing home for some days. Desai will use that time to make all the arrangements.

He stands beside Ila. He's given her the bedpan once, fed her Horlicks once. Mouth agape, snoring, she's sound asleep.

Can one ever imagine that once upon a time every head would turn when Ila walked past?

Desai takes a Calmpose after many years. Falls asleep on the swing, his legs folded under him.

The fan turns, the air cooler whirs, the swing moves to and fro.

If, even after all this, things boomerang, then he'll just have to tell the truth. And let matters take their course.

Sleep, come to me, sleep, come, come, sleep . . .

But sleep stays away.

Ila is his whole life. Who will he spend the rest of his life with? Who can tell him? The swing rocks gently to and fro.

*

According to Arjun-babu, it was still only late evening. But his friends drag him to his feet.

–Hey, got to go home.

–This early?

–It's two in the morning!

–Dhush! Nonsense!

–No more, come on, let's go home.

–Dhush! Kumkum isn't at home.

–C'mon. Home. Got to go home.

They have to help him to his feet. A group of drunks trying to lift another drunk is no easy matter. However, his friends refuse to give up.

Kumkum! Kumkum!

He went to see Kumkum today. Of course, he went to Keshtokali before that. What a cross-examination!

–You're saying it happened just like that?

–That's what she said.

–Or did you slip her some roots and herbs?

–No, no!

–Look—

–Why're you fussing so much?

–With medicine, a little here or there . . . even if something goes wrong, the abortion can still . . .

–No, I don't think it was like that.

–You know best. But don't come running to me after this.

–I won't need to.

–Better not.

–I'm off to see Kumkum.

–In the morning?

–May as well. You know her whims and fancies.

Really, the way Kumkum had acted today was absolutely the limit! As if she was a forest of flowers! A forest in which the first bud had just bloomed.

–Take me with you today!

–Where?

–Back to my flat. Just for a day.

–What about my work?

–You can drop me off and then carry on.

–Don't be crazy.

–I really, really want to.

–So do I.

Arjun-babu now rattles off lie after lie. Today he's free of the Jamuna-burden, tonight he'll get piss-drunk, make merry. If he gets trapped in Kumkum's whims, everything will be ruined.

–Without you there, I just don't feel like going home.

–Come, let's go one day.

–Arrey, here you're surrounded by love and care, always under your mother's eye. That flat can hardly be called a home!

–Why? Aren't they doing their work properly?

–Off and on. Without the lady of the house, things don't run as smoothly.

–Jamuna's not doing her work either?

–She hasn't even turned up today.

–We give her so much, but still . . .

–Mohini's cooking is inedible.

–Bahadur?

–Bahadur is fine.

–One by one, I'll sack them all.

–And do all the work yourself or what?

–I'll hire fresh staff.

–You won't be able to. With baby Koushik lying beside you, how will you?

–Not Koushik, Ameya.

–No. Kumkum's son Koushik.

–Arjun's son Ameya.

–Then he'll be named Arkadeb.

–No, that sounds terrible.

–I can see that you'll turn that boy into a monkey with your pampering, the way you're carrying on already.

–You'll be one who pampers him.

–Kumkum, I've been pampering you for ten years, have you turned into a monkey?

Kumkum seems to dissolve in delight. Sips her sherbet like a pampered little doll. Then resumes her tantrum.

–If you won't take me, Bapi will drop me. Won't you, Bapi?

Judge-sahib says, I won't drop you off. But if you're a really good girl, one day I could take you to visit.

Arjun asks him, in the next room, Will you really take her for a visit?

–No. But I don't want to refuse point-blank. At such a time, if anything upsets her . . .

–She's become a child herself.

–Absolutely. As if she's my little Mim again.

Little Mim! What horseshit! A thirty-five-year-old bundle, that too eight months pregnant . . . Mim!

–She's been acting so childish!

–Very. Listen, you better celebrate your wedding anniversary.

–You also think I should?

–We all think you should.

Runujhunu says, And think about a house as well. They've spent their childhood in big, roomy houses . . .

Arjun wants to say, No need for a house. The flat is big enough. I've crawled around it myself, there's plenty of space.

He says nothing.

It was while crawling about that he'd discovered Jamuna.

And then . . . then . . .

–Yes. I'll start asking around about a house.

*

If Desai had been a regular reader of crime fiction, the whole thing wouldn't have been so convoluted for him. Those who read Hadley Chase, they don't get so rattled. Although of course no one wants a murdered Jamuna in their bathtub.

Eyes shut, he keeps repeating, Forgive me. Forgive me, Mohsin, forgive me. I've never done anything like this before.

Because before this Ila hadn't murdered Jamuna. Ila hadn't put Jamuna in the bathtub. So I hadn't burdened you with Jamuna's dead body.

What if Ila isn't appeased? What if she does something like this again?

For now, let her be admitted into Surit Gupta's nursing home. Then I'll take her to Bombay.

Of course, the son will say, Don't be so focused only on Ma, Baba. She's not Ma any more. She's a stranger now. She's suspicious even of you.

Easy to say, Sukesh. Not so easy to do. What do you care if your mother lives or dies? We gave you an excellent education. You went abroad, married a white woman, made a life for yourself in Bombay, have children of your own. Your life will carry on just fine without your father and mother.

Suchetana studied, completed her degree. Then stayed at home for a couple of years. Her mother-in-law selected her for her only son, got them married.

We knew it would be just the two of us, so we planned our life that way. Your mother was involved in many things, I also had my work. But we made time to go out together, eat together, watch television together. It was such a lovely life.

Your mother would say, No one can be as happy as we are.

And we truly were happy. I would give thanks to the Lord every day. How often I thanked him!

Early that morning, that trunk call, who knew it would be you, breaking the news about Suchetana?

Even after that, the two of us, we had each other—how was I to know that Ila would lose her mind?

Now I feel that Ila is a traitor. Saying 'I'll kill you' is one thing, actually killing someone is something else entirely. What did you give her, Ila? Where did you get it? In a locality like this, money can buy you anything. Were you thinking of suicide? Then why didn't you do it? You and I would both have been saved.

Go, go to Surit's nursing home tomorrow. I'll make a thorough search.

He sits brooding, swinging, brooding, swinging. Suddenly he hears a drunken voice near the gate, raised energetically in song: *In this world, brother, anything is possible, it's true, it's tru–u–e!*

Arjun-babu's voice.

The name 'Barnamala' glows, neon-bright.

Outside the circle of light, Arjun's slurred voice is singing, *In this world, brother, anything is possible, it's true, it's tru–u–e!* A very drunk voice. A happy, happy man. Singing.

In fact, Arjun had spent a long time trying to recall this song. From his in-laws' all the way to Mandolina—Man-do-li-na!

Kapoor, Ghosh, Dutta, Malhotra—tonight had been a grand night because they'd all joined him.

Kapoor doesn't lose his head even after glugging down the Bay of Bengal. The secret to this mystery—consumption of Vitamin B, butter! Line your stomach first, then drink as much as you like!

Kapoor sticks his head out of the car: Hey, go home!

–Where are you going?

–For some fresh air, then home.

–And me? Don't leave me!

–Great. Hop in. Just one hour. Then back.

The durwan asks, Babu, won't you go inside?

Arjun clutches the durwan's beard and gives him a kiss. Says, The night is still a girl, my man! Let her become a young woman, let her youth brim over, then I'll come back home.

Kapoor pulls him into the car.

Dutt says, Doing poetry now!

–Of course! Want to hear?

–Just don't sing, that's all.

–Why shouldn't I?

The car took off. On such a night, in such a locality, only Kapoor would dare take the air!

A high-up police officer, how brave he is! Kapoor says, When can you enjoy Kolkata's clean, fresh air except at night?

–Kolkata is a head-shaved whore!

–Kolkata is a mystery.

–Kolkata is—Kolkata!

–Let's sing that song! Kolkata, Kolkata, Who says you don't matter?

Kapoor says, Shh, not so loud! Not in this neighbourhood.

A bunch of drunks. The driver drives on, stony faced. He has no choice. By the time each passenger is dropped off, it will be daylight.

By the time he can go to sleep, it will be nine in the morning. And Kapoor will come down in his shiny uniform sharp at nine-thirty. If you cut up the man, you'll find only machine parts, no flesh and blood.

The driver likes Arjun-babu. He often gives him big tips.

Drunkards of varying degree. Cool-headed driver. The gleaming car makes rounds of the maidan, searching for pollution-free air.

*

Mohsin opened the door, saw Jamuna and immediately threw up in a flowerpot. Some time has passed since then.

Near-dark corridor, a few potted plants. Those plants that don't thrive on the balcony, they're exiled here.

Stinking, belly bloated. After a murder, it is customary to slit open the belly before throwing the corpse into water. Or else the belly swells up, the body floats.

This is not the Jamuna of his dreams, but it's Jamuna nevertheless. Mohsin's feelings of love are overlaid with a fear of danger. And anger, furious anger.

First seduce her . . . Then murder her . . . Then try to put the handcuffs on me . . .

The tobacco-company-guesthouse's love-struck Mohsin vanishes. The one-time dockside fighter Mohsin swallows that Mohsin and transforms into Superman. Cunning, cruelty and efficiency in every pore.

Who needs Captain Singh?

He feels around her flaccid breasts and pulls out a hanky.

Alas, how flawlessly plump her breasts had been in his dream!

Tied up in the hanky are a bunch of keys, some money and a single key.

Yes, babu! You always left one of your keys with her, didn't you. Even if you hadn't, what difference would it have made? Jimmying open your door is child's play for Mohsin.

So, babu, your wife will have a child. You'll celebrate, you'll hand out sweets, you'll be so happy . . . And Jamuna, she'll be gone forever.

Why, babu? Your child in your wife's belly, in your maid's belly too—so deal with it!

In Mohsin's view, there's not much room for sympathy.

Jamuna, Jamuna! Did babu ever lay you down on his wife's bed? Mohsin will do so. Belly swollen with gas, oh lord, she looks pregnant.

Come, Jamuna, to the bridal chamber.

Dragging, dragging . . . dragging, dragging . . . bathroom, guestroom, bedroom. What a bed, my god! Satin sheets, satin pillows, such luxury! Fancy old cow you've become, Jamuna!

Up, onto the bed. Wait, let me pour all their perfumes on you. Pull the sheet over you. Wow, Jamuna, wow!

Lie there, belly-up—you'll get justice.

And if you get justice, the babus may get a little scared.

And the maids live a little longer.

This is the justice of the docks and ports, of Kolkata's dark underworld.

This is justice without judge, high court or supreme court. Without any wheeling-dealing in the name of the law.

Mohsin wipes down the door with the hanky. Let traces of Jamuna's body fluids remain on the bathroom floor. Let them stay outside the door too.

Mohsin mops his own corridor with phenyl. The key is near Jamuna. Now for a bath.

At the sound of him bathing, the writer comes out, surprised.

–You're bathing?

–Yes, babu. I felt very hot. When I can't sleep, I feel hot.

Mohsin smiles.

–You go to sleep, babu.

–It's three o' clock. No point sleeping now. Make some coffee. We'll both have some.

–Sure.

–Shall I open the balcony door?

–Here, I'll do it.

–If we sit here, we can see the sun rise, isn't that so?

–You can't see it, but you can tell.

–How cool it is!

–This flat is so high up!

–Maybe because there are so many trees . . .

–I'll get the coffee, babu.

The writer sits down. Mohsin's gloom has lifted. Good. He's a good man. Must tell my friend. Mohsin and Jamuna— why, this can be a story for the magazine's Puja-special issue!

He'll have to put Mohsin and Jamuna in another setting. Jute mill, railway yard, Sunderbans, and finally they'll triumph over it all and live happy ever after.

Not bad, not bad. Actually, anything can be material for a writer. The fragrance of coffee, a pack of Benson and Hedges, a few hours before the dawn, how amazing the sky looks! How many different kinds of sky I've seen, in how many places!

Suddenly, an old melody wafts through the air. *In this world, brother, anything is possible, it's true, it's tru–u–e!*

Ah, Chhabi Biswas! Such an old film, such an old film! Who's singing this song here, in Barnamala?

Mohsin says, Arjun-babu.

–So late at night? I've never . . .

–Happens sometimes, babu.

–That's bound to be.

*

Arjun is helped into the lift by the durwan, dropped off at his door.

–Oh! I can manage, I can manage. What do you think? I can manage just fine. I'm not drunk, dear man! Now just look at that! The security guard in front of my door—fast asleep! This is the problem. Pay the company a thousand bucks a month, and the guard just sleeps! Must tell them tomorrow itself.

The cosmos is wheeling through his head. With great difficulty he finally opens the door, enters, shuts it behind him.

Everything is spinning. His head is Solaris. He tiptoes into the bedroom and—what is that?!

Kumkum, Kumkum?! So you came after all? Fast asleep, all wrapped up in the sheets? Why didn't you switch on the air conditioner? You love sleeping in a cool room. Let me switch it on.

No, Kumkum. This won't do. You'll have to go back there first thing in the morning.

To stay here at this time . . .

Everything's spinning, spinning.

What a stubborn woman she is!

Arjun lies down on this edge of the bed. Falls asleep at once. The strong smell of perfume, other smells—nothing bothers him in the slightest. As he slips into slumber, he thinks: eight months or nine? Why is the stomach so big? Ameya, Koushik, Arkadeb, kiss kiss, kuss kuss, kiss kiss, Kumkum, Arjun is asleep, his mouth open wide.

TEN

A lot, a lot of alcohol; then, in the end, in a reckless mood, a tablet too; as a result, Arjun sleeps the sleep of the dead.

On the vast bed, Jamuna on one side, him on the other. The sun rises, hours pass, Arjun remains oblivious to it all.

Bahadur comes to work at this house first. He calls out, rings the bell over and over, but there's no response from babu.

Mohini comes just after Bahadur.

Again all the calling out, again the ringing of the doorbell. Mohini says, This is the slumber of Kumbhakaran himself!

Bahadur says, He doesn't usually sleep like this.

The liftman says, Arrey, he came home fully drunk at four in the morning! Passed out from the booze. Bound to be! Baap re! How much he must've drunk!

Mohini says, I'll go to No. 22 first, finish off there, then come back.

Bahadur says, Mohini, isn't the pest control due today? It will be a problem. Why isn't babu waking up?

—So what can I do about the pest control? Oof, Bahadur, you're too much!

—Jamuna hasn't come either.

—What do I know?

–Isn't there a terrible stink coming from somewhere?

–Where?

–How can you tell, Mohini? You stuffed yourself so full of fish and meat last night that your nostrils are bunged up.

–Get lost, boy. Babu told me to take it all, so I did.

Just then Desai emerges, holding Ila. He has bathed her, fed her, combed her hair, dressed her. They all fall silent.

Desai is talking to Ila. We're going out, Ila, you'll see what a beautiful place it is. We're going out, you'll see what a beautiful place it is.

–We're going to a beautiful place?

–Yes, Ila.

The doctor is with them. He goes towards the lift. Ila stares at Desai again.

–Why am I in a sari?

–Because you're going out, of course!

–When will we come back?

–Very . . . soon.

Tears drip from Desai's eyes. Still, he keeps talking: You'll see so many flowers . . . so many birds . . . you'll really love it . . .

They get into the lift. Desai has a bag slung over his shoulder. Tears flow continuously from his eyes.

Mohini folds her palms and touches them to her forehead.

–Just seeing them is a blessing, a blessing. How many lifetimes of penance the mad woman's done to get a husband like that! Ever seen a husband put up with so much from his wife?

Doesn't drink, doesn't lust after women, it's just his wife, his wife and his wife. Given his life for her.

The sweeper says, with heartfelt sorrow, He won't keep Memsahib here. He'll put her in a Bombay hospital. And then do you think sahib will stay here, all alone?

–Where will he go?

–To his son, in Bombay.

–Just the one daughter, and she too died. Sahib is such a good man. Born to suffer.

Mohini says, They're both good people. She may be crazy but she's bighearted. But what's up with this house? Babu just isn't opening the door!

Bahadur asks, Hasn't Jamuna come today either?

Mohini shrugs.

Arjun-babu is fast asleep. The air conditioner's on, the room is cool, so cool. Deep in sleep, he has no dreams, no worries.

*

Around 10 o'clock, Mohsin sees the sweeper standing outside No. 9.

–What's the matter, jamadar?

–Mohsin!

–What is it?

–Are you getting a bad smell?

–No.

–How strange! I was working in No. 7, but there's such a bad smell coming from No. 9 . . .

–You should tell the Office.

–You can't smell it?

–No, my friend. I have a guest, you know? And the boss is bringing a few more along. There's so much to do. Get Chinese food, get bottles of beer, Jamuna hasn't come either, so I've got to clean the rooms, tidy everything . . .

Mohsin leaves. The sweeper can't decide what to do. Finally, he goes to the Office. If there's something amiss, it would be wrong not to inform the Office. Babu isn't responding, and then there's that smell . . .

It's a smell the sweeper knows only too well, which is why he is so astonished. Babu got in early this morning, and he was dead already, rotting already?

At the Office he finds not the manager but the caretaker, Uday-babu. The manager has stepped out. It's Uday-babu who had got the sweeper this job.

–Uday-babu!

–What is it, Ruplal?

–Terrible smell coming from No. 9.

–But there's no one in No. 9!

–How come, babu?

–Arrey, the missus is at her parents'. And just yesterday morning Arjun-babu said he was going to Haldia for a few days. So who could be in the flat?

–Babu came back at four this morning, very drunk. The durwan will know, babu . . .

–What's it to you, Ruplal? And if he only got back around four o'clock, very drunk . . .

–He's not opening the door. Mohini and Bahadur both kept ringing the bell . . .

–Must be asleep.

–But the smell . . .

–It must be something like what happened that time in No. 21. They left a whole fish lying in the bag and went off to Delhi, remember? The fish began to rot . . . we broke down the door and then felt so foolish!

–Babu, this is not a rotten-fish smell. Anyway, let it be. I've done my duty, I've told you.

–Do you work in that house?

–Chaman works there. He's on leave, so I'm doing it. But I couldn't even get in today.

–Let me see, let me see. The phone's ringing again! Wait. Yes, Office. Yes, Mrs Choudhury, I have informed the plumber. He'll come soon, and I'll escort him to you myself. Yes, good-bye. Ruplal!

–Babu!

–No. 17 needs a plumber, in No. 13 a switch isn't working, in No. 10 they don't have water, you're saying there's a smell coming from No. 9 . . . OK, I've noted it down. Let the manager come, I'll tell him . . .

–OK, babu.

Mohsin comes in.

–Now what do you want, Mohsin?

–Could Manager-sahib please come upstairs? The boss is coming. He wants to repaint the place, wants to talk.

–Your boss is really something! Spends company money to paint the house every year!

–Yes, babu.

–Wait, let me write this down as well. I can't remember everything, it's simply not possible. Stench from No. 9 . . . Manager to go to No. 11. What did Desai-sahib say? Oh, to keep an eye on his flat. And what else? What else?

Mohsin and Ruplal walk out. Mohsin is filled with impatience, impatience for revenge. When will everyone break into No. 9?

Yesterday Jamuna was cool to the touch, so cool. Had someone kept her on ice, then? Where?

Mohsin goes over everything carefully in his mind. Left her key lying next to Jamuna, and shut every door in No. 9. Wiped his own corridor shiny clean as soon as it was dawn. Now Mohsin is busy, really busy. Boss is expected.

If the Jamuna matter could be exposed while everyone was here . . . Mohsin waits in front of the lift.

Uday-babu yells, What a king's job you have, Mohsin! Ordering flowers, booze, meals, all on the telephone . . .

–Yes, babu.

Mohsin thinks, And you lot are skimming cash off maintenance, babu!

Achha, how come no one from Jamuna's slums has come to ask about her? This is what happens when you have no one to call your own.

And what are Johnny and Tala up to? Haven't they heard about Mohsin looking for Jamuna? Why haven't they come? Ghulam's mother, she hasn't come either?

Poor Jamuna! You used to say that these were all your people. No one, my dear, no one! If you did have someone, wouldn't they have come?

But don't worry, Jamuna. The man who's ruined you, I've made sure to fix him.

Made v–e–ry sure!

*

Meanwhile, at the slum, Johnny and Tala are in a dilemma. They've guessed that something's amiss, but can't say anything to anyone.

Moloy, Jamuna's husband, is the one who stirs things up.

His factory has reopened. The union and the management have come to an agreement. Moloy and the others have been paid some of their dues. It's a mere pittance, a measly three hundred rupees.

Still, Moloy has kept his word. He had said he would come for Jamuna as soon as he got his money. If she still wants him, let her come with him to Beleghata. Moloy has even found them a place to stay.

Why is there no trace of Jamuna?

–Jamuna's not at home?

–As you can see.

–Don't you know anything? Where is she?

–How should we know? She went to work. We went to the movies, a mehfil, then went to sleep, and now as you can see we're drinking tea.

–If you don't know, who does?

–Moloy! All this time we were lowly insects to you. We disgusted you, you told Jamuna over and over, don't hang out with them. And now suddenly you have such faith in us? Get lost! You half-gent! Why didn't you ask after your wife all this time? Where were you?

Ghulam's mother was fetching water. She lowered her pitcher and said, Who's that? Is it Moloy?

–Yes, it's me.

–Are you talking about Jamuna? She hasn't come home, hasn't gone to work, since day-before-yesterday evening. Mohsin came looking for her yesterday morning. She's not at work, not at home, so where is she?

–She hasn't gone to work since day before yesterday evening?

–That's what he said. And where were you all this time, dear boy? Left your wife all alone for so long?

–Do you know where she is?

–Did she tell me, that I should know?

Johnny and Tala exchange glances. Some silent message passes between them, but Moloy can't quite tell what.

–Moloy, come this way, we need to talk.

–Let me open the room first.

–Got a key?

–She gave me a key . . .

The room silently tells him so much. The cot covered with a bamboo mat, the pitcher filled with water, the saucepan face down beside a sparkling clean Janta stove, a tin of rice next to it, a wire basket full of potatoes. Cockroaches crawling all over them.

Jamuna would say, Who knows when you'll show up. At least I can make you some boiled rice and potatoes!

Johnny says, You've no idea what a woman you had. A slum girl! As if all the gentlewomen are chaste virgins! She kept everything ready to feed you, just in case you showed up. When she went to work, she'd give her key to Ghulam's mother and say, Mashi, I've got everything for him. Even if he's lost his key, he can get in and rest. Tell him to wait inside.

Tala says, Whenever she got something nice, she'd always bring it for you.

Moloy's lungi and vest are lying washed and ready. He breaks open her trunk. Clothing, more clothing . . . and what's this, so much cash?

–So much money? Fourteen hundred?

–Why not? Worked four houses, earned four hundred and fifty. Thirty rupees room rent. Everything else, her food, clothing, she got from the babus.

–Saved every paisa, so when her gentleman husband returned, they could set up shop together.

–But where has she gone, leaving behind all this?

–That's the question. Make some tea, Tala.

Tala makes tea. Johnny shuts the door. They'll have to tell Moloy everything, except the bit about money in the lopt. One can't really trust a half-gent. And they hadn't gone last evening as Jamuna had instructed them to, after all. They had guessed what had happened.

They hadn't gone to the movies either. They had been beating up Lame Doctor.

Lame Doctor had himself come rushing to them.

–Go, you two, go! I've given Jamuna the wrong stuff by mistake, I've messed up bad!

–Meaning?

–I was stoned. Messed up bad.

–You mean you've given her the deathly dose?

–Yes!

–Will she die?

–Take it she's dead already.

–Bloody hell!

–Go quick, you two!

–What's the use of our going?

–Take her to a hospital!

–How?

–The bitch will die!

–And you'll live, eh? Get lost, you bastard! Can we go to a place like that and look for her? Isn't it a murder case now? The police, the employer, they'll hang us!

–What will you do to me?

–Screw your doctoring forever.

They had gone crazy with rage. With grief for Jamuna. The thought that their 'lopt money' plan for freedom had failed filled them with frustrated fury.

–We'll break your bones, squeeze every paisa you own, throw you out of here!

–If Jamuna dies, you'll . . .

–You've ruined our lives, you bastard! Didn't you see what medicine you were dishing out?

They took Lame Doctor to his room, thrashed him soundly, broke his bones, smashed open his strongbox and took all his money.

They don't tell Moloy everything. They leave out the bit about Lame Doctor's medicine. But they tell him the rest.

–Jamuna was pregnant?

–That Arjun-babu's doing.

–A tough woman like Jamuna!

–A woman, after all! How tough could she be?

–She's gone to that same babu's place?

–She said she was.

–You guys telling the truth?

–You think we're lying?

–We never laid a finger on her . . .

–Who gave her to you in marriage?

–Both of you.

–She was a really close friend.

–Jamuna would say the same thing.

–This much is true, that she would bring us information and we would do our thing.

–And then you, you bastard, you preached your 'honest living' line. So after she married you, she did just that. Stopped giving us news for jobs.

–Is there something wrong with an honest living?

–We can never see eye to eye with you. Always despised us, and lived off Jamuna yet tried to make her a half-gent too, you bastard! Who doesn't have to work hard? You think our work isn't hard? Don't we slog?

–Don't call me a half-gent.

–Why shouldn't we? Jamuna earned four hundred and fifty, you'll get five hundred at most. Even in a slum, that's not enough to live on! And yet you put on such gentrified airs!

–Where did she go?

–What to say? She had a terrible tongue. Poisonous as a snake. Day before yesterday she went to Arjun-babu's in the morning, really swore at him. Said, You're the sinner, you sort this out. That evening she left saying, Babu says he's making the arrangements, so I'm going. Or how will I face Moloy when he comes?

–She went to Arjun-babu's house?

–That's what she said.

–She had a key . . . to get in and work . . . I remember now.

–Go there, you're her husband after all!

–She didn't work only in that one house.

–She worked in four.

–Should I go there too?

–What's the point? Arjun-babu, flat No. 9. His wife has gone to her parents' to have her child. Jamuna told us everything.

–You come too.

–Why should we come?

–You're the witnesses!

–We, your witnesses?! Daroga-babu will die laughing. Now you're being funny, Moloy.

–Why?

–In your eyes we're good-for-nothings. In the Daroga's eyes, we are minor goondas. If they take us to the police station and thrash us, our boss won't bother to come and save us.

–I'll go alone?

–Why not? You're her husband. You have a right to ask.

–Going alone, somehow . . .

–That babu needs to be punished. Bastard's made of money. Has a wife at home. But chases his maid . . .

–Not just that flat, I would have forbidden her to work anywhere in that building!

–This is what I call babu-bullshit! You won't bring home a bloody paisa, she'll slog away as a maid, and even there you'll shove your damn husbandhood on her!

Tala snaps, What other work is there in this locality? Won't peddle cocaine, won't sell hooch, won't work as a maid, then what will she do?

–Honest hard work . . .

–Don't talk rubbish! I'll smash your face. Honest living, hard work! Just listen to our Reverend High Priest!

–You knew bloody well where she lived, what she did, who she hung out with, why did you marry her? What did you think—you'd marry her and she'd take you all the way up to Park Street?

–No, no, not that. But I know that Jamuna always dreamt of big money.

–And why shouldn't she? Honest girl. Young woman. Eat well, dress well, watch television, live in a nice home—yes, she had dreams. And you've got to act the bastard about that too?

–Never mind. I'd better be going now . . .

–What're you picking up your bag for? Moloy?

–Moloy, if you think that we'll get caught because of your wife, while you slip away, then you're still in your mother's womb!

–Hey Moloy! We'll finish you ourselves! Bloody bastard!

–I'm putting my bag down.

–Leave it here. We'll lock the door. We'll keep the key. We don't trust you.

–Look, Johnny, look at Moloy's face! The bastard's petrified!

–We're going for Jamuna's sake, brother, not his. Come, let's go and watch the fun.

*

By the time they enter Barnamala, it's around one in the afternoon. Moloy looks around nervously. He's never set foot in here before. Never thought he would. For Jamuna's sake . . .

At the sight of Johnny and Tala, Captain Singh winks, smiles.

–What news, friends?

–What news can we give you, dada? Come here. This is Moloy.

–Moloy! Moloy who?

–Jamuna's husband.

–Jamuna's husband? He he he, how amazing is that! I know Jamuna, but never seen her husband. So what's he want, Jamuna's husband?

–He's looking for Jamuna.

–Of course he should. It's a husband's right to look. Mohsin's looking, Desai-sahib's looking, No. 21's not here, of course, but No. 9's Mohini's been saying Jamuna's not come. That girl came here day before yesterday for sure. Saw her myself.

Moloy says, She told everyone she was going to No. 9.

–Of course she would. She works there.

–You don't understand. After that, she never came home.

–Mohsin said . . . Hang on, come to Manager-babu's room. No. 9 . . . Manager-babu has been told about the bad smell from No. 9. Just now they were talking about what could be the cause.

The manager's instant response was: No. 9's babu is not at home.

Captain says, What d'you mean? Just this morning at four o' clock babu came back totally drunk—ask the liftman. How much Mohini, Bahadur, called out when they came!

–Your wife couldn't have gone to No. 9 in the evening. The flat was empty then.

The manager is fully aware of who's man Captain really is.

Captain says, Jamuna always carried a key to the flat.

–How is that possible?

–Babu gave it to her. Call Mohsin, no, he'll tell you more.

–Go to Mohsin's flat and talk to him. He's expecting his top boss, he can't come down now.

–You won't come with us?

–You go, why don't you.

–No babu, you come too.

–And will they come as well?

–Why not? Like brothers to Jamuna, I know them very well. What, Johnny, isn't that so?

–What can we say, dada! She told everyone she was going to Arjun-babu's flat, to No. 9. After that . . .

–When did she tell you?

–Day before yesterday, Manager-babu.

–And you've come to enquire only today?

–Yesterday, we weren't here. Her husband was also busy in his factory these last two days.

–Who knows where she's gone!

Moloy says, What d'you mean? Shouldn't we first see where she told everyone she was coming?

Ergo, everyone enters the lift. Johnny and Tala think, We missed out on the lopt loot, but at least, thanks to Jamuna, we got a ride in this lift!

Mohsin at No. 11 is busy, very busy. Yet he comes out to meet them.

–What's happened, babu?

–This is Jamuna's husband. Come to look for her. It seems Jamuna came here day before?

Captain says, Of course she did.

Mohsin says, She came late afternoon, day before. Said, I'm not feeling well, won't work today. Said, I have the key to No. 9, I'll go there and rest a bit.

–She said so?

–She said so.

–Then?

–Then, yesterday morning, she didn't show up to work. So I told Bahadur at No. 9: I have a guest staying. I have to be at his beck and call. I am alone. Bahadur said, she hadn't gone there. No. 9 babu checked with Desai-babu, but she hadn't gone there either. And today, she hasn't come to us.

–No. 9?

–No idea, babu. But Bahadur said, they hadn't been able to get in this morning. Babu just wouldn't open the door.

–Desai-sa'ab . . .

–He left this morning with memsahib for the hospital.

Manager says, Understood. OK, you go back to work.

Mohsin's boss comes out. He's very annoyed.

–Manager!

–Yes, sir!

–Find out what's rotting in No. 9. Very bad smell coming! I smelt it as soon as I arrived. What is this? I'm expecting more guests today. What a stink!

–Yes, sir, at once.

Captain says, Haven't you heard, babu? Ruplal said, the No. 7 maid said, there's a terrible stink from there.

–All right, all right, I'll have a look.

They all troop across to Avantika.

Yes, there is a stench from somewhere. A faint, strangely familiar smell. A smell that carries in it death, rotting corpses, much more.

The doorbell rings and rings. Then begins the banging on the door.

Arjun-babu was surfacing from the depths of sleep. As if floating up from the bottom of the ocean. He was being awakened by Jamuna. Because his breath was being assailed by the stench of Jamuna's puff-bellied rotting body.

Arjun-babu staggers to his feet. He can barely open his eyes, he's pissed himself, his dhoti is soaked—but why is it stinking so much?

Kumkum! Kumkum!

Someone's shouting outside. Banging on the door . . . Shocking! Banging, what audacity! They dare to bang on his door?

Shaking his head, he lurches to the door, opens it. The stench takes over, is everywhere.

–What? Who are you?

–Arjun-babu, this is—

–Where's Jamuna?

–Who the hell are you?

–Jamuna's husband.

–Jamuna's husband? So how am I to know where she is?! Oh, what a stink! Chhi chhi, such a stink . . .

Manager says, The smell's coming from your flat, sir. I've been getting reports about it from 10 a.m. Tried ringing the bell, couldn't wake you, so . . .

Moloy says, We're coming in.

–No, you're not. My wife's in that room. No one can go in.

–We're all coming in.

Captain says, I'm going in, sa'ab. Manager too.

Manager asks, What's stinking so much?

Arjun-babu yawns, staggers. The stink, it really is . . .

–What's that smell, Manager?

They all enter the flat. The stench is everywhere, even in the bedroom.

They enter the bedroom.

–What's this?! Who is this?

Arjun-babu is now a mere spectator. Kumkum, Kumkum had wanted to come . . . I slept beside Kumkum . . . Kumkum!

Captain flips back the satin sheet. It's swollen-bellied, rotting-fleshed Jamuna. Fluids oozing out of every pore. Her face is bloated, her teeth stick out. The smell, the smell, the overpowering smell.

Arjun-babu lets out a terrible scream. No, that's not Jamuna! It can't be Jamuna! I moved her out day before yesterday night. Desai! Desai knows!

Manager says, Desai returned from Bombay early yesterday morning. Stop, don't say another word. Chhi, chhi, chhi!! Barnamala's good name is sunk. I'm calling the police station.

–It's not Jamuna! Not Jamuna!

–Captain, keep an eye on him. Chhi, chhi, Arjun-babu!

–She didn't just work in my house. Other flats too . . .

–You were sleeping next to her, what are you blabbering about now?

Captain grabs him. Says, Don't move, babu! Chhi, chhi! Sleeping next to a dead body?

–It was Kumkum lying there!

–And she turned into Jamuna?! Amazing! Never heard the like!

Hordes of people crowd in. Barnamala had never seen such a catastrophe. Evil deeds had always been covered up here. Never revealed themselves like this.

Arjun weeps copiously. His life, his world, his household, his reputation, his contracts, his black money, his married life, everything is drowning in this rotten stench.

Jamuna gleefully bares her teeth, sees everything, keeps oozing fluids, spreading the stench.

Arjun-babu passes out.

Translator's Afterword

This urban novella set in Kolkata in the mid 1980s grabbed my attention as a translator right away. There was the signature Mahasweta Devi tone—dry, sardonic, trenchant, funny; the sharp eye for the phony or hypocritical; a broad ensemble of characters drawn with a scalpel-sharp pen; and a clear-eyed understanding of the ways of a hierarchical, stratified society. The close to farcical story-line—murder? urban crime story? morality tale?—moves along at a fast clip, as the events unfold over roughly 48 hours.

As a translator, the multiple registers of spoken language were a challenge. One understood immediately whether those speaking were Bengali or not, which class segment they belonged to, what level of education they had, formal or informal, and, of course, aspects of character and personality. All of this without any further explanation by the author. The flattening effect of English (twee choices like broad cockney being unacceptable to this translator) is regrettable. It is one of the limitations of translation.

I was also both appreciative of and challenged by another distinct feature of Mahasweta Devi's writing. There is a certain ease of reference and assumption that her readers would pick up on her cultural allusions, scraps of song, lines from poems, humorous digs and playful puns. She assumes a community. The opening line of the story exemplifies this—it comes with a set of assumptions expressed in a throwaway manner: that we would understand why Khidirpur as a locality may warrant a certain reaction; that we would appreciate the irony of gleaming skyscraper apartments for the elite shooting up here.

And yet neither does she try to make things easy: many of her characters use insider street slang and graphically explicit abuses which would be unfamiliar to the genteel or middle-class reader. This is a political choice Mahasweta Devi articulates elsewhere. It is not her intention to 'explain' to her readers: they need to put in the effort to catch on, and keep up. Ignorance is privilege, the way she sees it.

A note about process. My knowledge of the language of origin, Bengali, is far from good. I read the script, and I always translate directly from the original, but my grasp of usage, idioms, vocabulary, leaves much to be desired. Yet I am fussy about nuance, tone, over-reading or over-explaining; so I check my draft closely with knowledgeable friends as I work, constantly recalibrating, before submitting it. That is only step one. Step Two is the editorial contribution. In this case, this has been exemplary, both exhaustive and sensitive to the literary aspects of the original, and resulted in the opportunity for me to rethink and question my own choices, either accepting the alternative offered or pushing myself to come up with another. I cannot stress enough how important it is to have a capable reader/editor who, line by line, phrase by phrase, tests the translation against the original, identifies shortcomings and suggests corrections and improvements. A fresh eye, a second opinion—invaluable.

So I end by acknowledging with gratitude the important contribution made to this translation by Chittrovanu Mazumdar, who agreed to act as my first reader, sounding board and go-to consultant; Moinak Biswas, who patiently addressed queries which confounded us; and Sunandini Banerjee, who picked the whole text apart so that we could put it together again, new and improved. My salaams.

Translator's Notes

PAGE **1** | Swarming around a riverrine wet dock, '**Khidirpur**'—one of Kolkata's oldest neighbourhoods—is regarded as an abode of smuggling and other crimes.

PAGE **5** | '*Oh flower-filled forest path*': Lines from the Bengali song 'Banatal phuley-phuley dhaka', sung by Hemanta Mukherjee.

PAGE **7** | '**Arjun-babu's uncle**': The original text has the word 'baba' or father; this may be an error, or an indication of an older relative who is like a father.

PAGE **8** | '**she won't die . . . at her in-laws**' ': A reference to the many 'dowry deaths' in which women were persecuted and killed for their inability to fulfil their in-laws' monetary demands of their parents.

PAGE **11** | '**When an old cock . . . this is his fate.**': This proverb is also the title of a famous play *Buro Shaliker Ghare Ro* by well-known literary figure and playwright Michael Madhusudhan Dutt (1824–1873).

PAGE **16** | '**want to open a hotel**': Colloquial usage for a modest eatery, often a roadside shack serving food.

PAGE **17** | '**Oh, what an Arjun he is**': A sarcastic reference to the legendary warrior hero, prince Arjun, in the epic Mahabharata.

PAGE **18** | '**Joy Bangla**' was the sardonic name given to the epidemic of conjunctivis, an eye infection that swept Kolkata in 1971 and was widely attributed to the flood of refugees from the Bangladesh war of independence from

Pakistan. Refugee camps sprang up in and around the city of Calcutta as it was then called, and infectious and contagious diseases were rampant.

PAGE 22 | 'Indrapuri' is the capital of the heavenly kingdom in Hindu mythology.

PAGE 39 | 'Flowers, flowers! . . . Intoxicating the swarm of bees!': Lines from the Bengali song 'Ke nibi phool, ke nibi phool', written by Kazi Nazrul Islam. From the second line on, Mahasweta Devi either misremembers the original or deliberately creates her own adaptation.

PAGE 59 | 'dip in the Jamuna': Jamuna is the name of a river that joins the sacred Ganges. It is also venerated, like the Ganges.

PAGE 61 | 'head is full of Bhopal gas': A reference to the Bhopal gas tragedy on the night of 2–3 December 1984 at the Union Carbide India Limited (UCIL) pesticide plant in Bhopal, Madhya Pradesh, India when over 500,000 people in the small towns around the plant were exposed to the highly toxic gas.

PAGE 65 | 'my beautiful orchard': The original phrase, *sajano bagan*, is also the title of a famous play by Manoj Mitra (b. 1938).

PAGE 67 | 'Why did I not drench her in my tears': Line from the Bengali song 'Keno chokher joley bhijiye dilem na', written by Rabindranath Tagore.

PAGE 78 | 'Vinod Mehta' was a deputy commissioner of the Kolkata Police who was brutally murdered along with his bodyguard by smuggling cartels in Khidirpur in 1984.

PAGE **78** | '**Fancy Market**' is notorious the world over for its sundry smuggled, 'fancy' goods.

PAGE **88** | '**is thriving, is thriving, will thrive!**': In the original, the phrase is '*cholchhey, cholchhey, cholbey*', a chant common to political and protest processions.

PAGE **93** | '**Such lifetimes of penance . . . get a husband like this!**': This refers to a religious-cultural belief that a lifetime of penance can earn you a boon or ensure reincarnation as a more blessed being.

PAGE **102** | '**Kalighat wedding**': The Kali temple at Kalighat in Kolkata is considered a holy place for marriage, often by couples who seek the blessings of the goddess Kali for a quick and simple wedding.

PAGE **107** | '**The babu in No. 11's a good guy.**': The original contains an error. No 11 is the guesthouse where Mohsin works.

PAGE **120** | '*In this world, brother, anything is possible, it's true, it's tru–u–e!*': From the Bengali song 'Ei Duniyay Bhai Sabi Hoy', written and set to music by Salil Chowdhury, sung by Manna Dey in the Bengali film *Ekdin Ratre* [One night] (1956). As recreated in this novel, the film's protagonist, completely drunk, sings this song walking through the city.

PAGE **125** | '**Chhabi Biswas**' (1900–62) was a popular Bengali film actor.

PAGE **127** | '**Kumbhakaran**' is a character from the epic Mahabharata, brother of Ravana, cursed to sleep like one dead for months at a time.

PAGE **139** | '**Park Street**' is an elite neighbourhood in central Kolkata.